The Demoniac

© 2021 Genevieve St. Clair
St. Clair Publications

ISBN 978-1-947514-38-6

Printed in the United States of America

St. Clair Publications P. O. Box 726 Mc Minnville, TN 37111—0726

http://stclairpublications.com

Cover Design: Rebecca Rae Tansel

The Demoniac

Genevieve St. Clair

Acknowledgments

I am so thankful to God for giving me such an inquisitive nature. I love to think outside of the box and to create from nothing. This book is dedicated to God and His Love.

I am thankful for my friend Matt Jackson who spent long hours editing and re-editing as I changed and added to this book.

I am also thankful to my oldest son, Jimmy Dean Abalos, for spending several hours editing, suggesting better ways of wording and helping with my poor skills on the computer.

I am overjoyed with the amazing graphic design of my dear friend Rebecca Rae Tansel. Thank you for making this the best cover ever! You are so talented.

Thank you to my Daddy, Stan St. Clair for your patience, skills and understanding. I love you.

The Demoniac

Chapter 1

On a small stool before the treasured mirror Kallisto positioned her body sensually as Aphrodesia had trained her to do before leaving for Cyprus. "It is all about what men want to see upon entering a room. You need to cause their desire to ignite instantly."

Brushing slowly through her sumptuous black hair, she admired the glorious representation of Zeus almighty, his beautiful Callisto and the love they shared until Zeus' jealous wife Hera banished her to her final resting place in the heavens as the constellation, The Great Bear.

Her delicate fingers traced the constellation and she smiled as she recalled her mother's tender voice explaining to her that as an infant she had been named after Calisto but spelled Kallisto to honor Calisto but not to incur any displeasure from the gods. She was to be dedicated to the gods to be used in whichever way they chose, and that this would bring blessings to her family as well as securing her place in the heavens. She knew one day she would be a star in that constellation and others could look up and remember her.

"I saw this while traveling and knew someone created it just for you," Joseph said to her when she saw it for the first time. She had only been in Gerasa for a few months at that time, but it seemed that everyone knew of her. Most people pointed and whispered "hetaera,"* making it sound filthy when in fact it was a perfectly acceptable way of life.

"Kind sir, I don't believe I have the finances for such an exquisite piece of art." Plouton had kept his promise to meet all her needs however, luxuries were not necessary expenditures. There was the arrangement she had made with the instructor at the gymnasium to educate her in order to be an independent woman in time, and her kind lover, Petros gave her extra on occasion but, this was beyond her income.

"Kallisto, it belongs to no one save you. There is not another living soul that will treasure such a piece as it should be treasured." Joseph urged her to gaze upon her reflection as he explained the painstaking work that went into making it reflect the world so clearly. "It was created in the Orient and brought to Mt. Olympus for approval from your gods."

Not sure that she believed every word, it did deepen her desire to own it. She had not yet developed a penchant for bartering, so she began to walk away. "Kallisto, since it should be in your house, I will take only what you can afford." She looked carefully at his face to detect some sign of deceit yet found none. Quickly, she counted all she had and saved back only enough for some grain and olive oil. Eating only bread and lentils for a while seemed a fair trade for such a jewel. Daily she thanked Zeus for the opportunity to own such a luxurious item. She expected to see Joseph at her door requiring her services for additional payment, but it never happened.

Deep in thought she had not heard Plouton arrive, so his touch startled her back to reality. He was never gentle and always demanded silence from her. "Plouton, I know that you require silence," she began slowly and softly, "but, I have news today." His large hand covered her mouth as he growled in her ear, "Silence! If I wanted to hear a woman speak, I would stay at home." He continued in the usual ways and she allowed her mind to wander. Two days ago, it was confirmed that she was with child. Her first and only stop was at the temple of Artemis where she spoke to Aphrodesia. The conversation was not as comforting as she had hoped. They both knew that Plouton was certainly wealthy enough to maintain a second family, his pig farm was the largest in the Decapolis however, he was well known as a ruthless master to all in his employ.

Why was this child not that of Joseph or Petros? Joseph had never attempted to be with her. She had confronted him one day about that and he explained that it would be a disgrace to his god. She could not understand that concept, so she asked more questions. "Adonai, the God of Abraham, Isaac, and Jacob, Creator of the universe and all of mankind," she watched as he spoke about his God. His arms raised toward the sky expressing His grandeur.

"If this is so, why have I never heard of Him? Everyone knows Zeus is the greatest of all the gods. How does Adonai fit into the family of gods?"

Joseph laughed and said that Adonai was more powerful than any of the other gods. She pondered that for a long time. Her solitude created more questions. The gymnasium* taught of all other gods but, Adonai was never mentioned.

Petros was a kind and gentle lover. He was a philosopher and a sculptor. He told her that he would have made a statue of her, but her beauty would cause even Aphrodite to be inflamed with jealousy. She allowed a smile to cross her face at that thought and Plouton noticed.

"So! I have pleased you," Plouton said as he rose to dress.

"Plouton," she began again.

"Yes, yes, what do you want?" She took a deep breath and lowered her eyes as she slipped her peplos over her head. "Come on girl, I don't have much time." He never called her by name even though he had visited her regularly at the temple. She had assumed it was due to his obvious need to feel loved. He was cold and insensitive no matter the lengths she had gone to pour out the love of Aphrodite on him during their times of worship.

"Well, I have news I think you will be pleased to hear." He just stared angrily, "I am with child…" she paused for a moment to watch his reaction and catch her breath.

"Whore! Why do you burden me with such news? This could be anyone's child!"

"Plouton, no one else has ever released their seed in me, and there has only been one other man since we left Cyprus 4 years ago. This child is…" Intense burning in her face followed by the taste of blood came from the back of his hand. Her heart pounded, and her breath was taken as she slammed into the stone wall, which seconds ago had been across the room. Her body collapsed into a pile on the cold dirt floor, and she caught a glimpse of Plouton's departure as her eyes shut.

Awakened by the sunlight she tried unsuccessfully to move. People passed by her window and she imagined them to be on their way to the gymnasium, the temple or the marketplace. She considered calling out to anyone but, she knew that she would be ignored, hetaerae were outcasts. The solitude led to fear and tears as the pain increased until she slept once more.

Rousing from sleep the next day she was determined to rise. Slowly she inched her way toward the heavy wooden door, opening it slightly she called out to a woman passing by. "Please get a physician," was all she could get out before collapsing again. The woman ran to the temple to get a physician that would treat hetaerae. Rest and broth were ordered. Aphrodesia prepared some fish broth and helped Kallisto for the next several days. Having company helped her feel better. Her family was to arrive soon, and she hoped to be up and about for their annual visit.

The day finally arrived but only Desma and her mother came. A small disappointment since Kallisto looked forward to the time spent with all her siblings. She enjoyed three weeks with the two of them and then Desma was granted extra time to help Kallisto heal which slightly made up for not seeing everyone this year.

"Desma, I have a favor to ask of you," Kallisto spoke quietly.

"Anything!" Desma admired her sister for her faithfulness to the family and their gods. She had been told that because of her sister the entire household was blessed. "I have written several letters to my child in case I do not see him or her. I want it to know about me and the place assured to me among the stars of the Great Bear. I want this child to know and love the stories of our gods, and to look up and think of me." She sighed and smiled tenderly caressing her still flat stomach.

Desma's thoughts were suddenly frantic. She had not considered that as an option. What about the father? What about her own betrothal? Would she be expected to care for this child? Was she willing to do it?

"Desma, are you ok?" Kallisto understood her death to be a high probability. Along with the forgiveness and love she had given as a priestess she had received many diseases which led to a bad omen for births, many deaths were brought to women attempting motherhood in her profession. Hetaerae often lost their babies before birth or their own lives during birth. Only, in this moment she realized that Desma did not understand that. Desma nodded, unable to force a smile.

"Kallisto, I am to be married when I return home. Mother allowed me only 5 months to remain here while she finishes the preparations for my wedding." Kallisto smiled and squealed with delight as she jumped toward her younger sister. The two girls hugged.

"Do you know him well?"

"No," Desma admitted "but, his family is from Kanata and he was sent to Athens for studies."

"So, they have money!

"I guess so, he trained in mathematics and art. He heard about our family from George who he met at the gymnasium." Desma pondered the weight of the situations here and at home as the day grew short.

Chapter 2

Time passed swiftly. The sisters enjoyed every moment together. Shopping had become Desma's favorite activity. Short trips to the market for fish, olives, grain and figs or to pick out material in which to dress the child when it arrived. Kallisto especially cherished the time. Her entire life she had longed for such a friend to spend time with. Desma was so much like her mother, her slightly wider hips perfect for childbearing and strong arms necessary to run a good home properly. Her laugh was loud and honest where Kallisto restrained her joy as she had been trained to do. She asked many questions about life at home longing for the life she had been forced to miss out on.

"The child will be here soon." Kallisto announced as they finished breakfast one chilly morning. "It is cold but, the sun is shining, and I have decided to purchase a cradle." Desma laughed and strapped on her sandals immediately. "I noticed how much you enjoy the marketplace so be prepared to walk… a lot today. Also, I hope that Joseph is finally back since he would be the one most likely to have exactly what I want. And I want you to meet him. When I visit his shop, I feel a peace and somehow safe."

"In what way?" Desma wondered out loud.

"He is an especially kind man. He has never been rude or made any advances toward me. I imagine him like a father," Kallisto paused and thought before continuing. "One time, a woman began to say mean things about me, and he demanded that she stop. When she did not, he told her to leave his shop and he forbade her from purchasing anything from him that day." She smiled and sighed at the pleasure that brought. No one had ever been so considerate of her feelings. "Once a man remarked about my lifestyle and Joseph made him leave as well. He is like my guardian somehow." She looked at her sister and smiled at the fact that Desma did not likely have to contend with those scenarios. She looked toward the dirt road in front of them and twirled around like a child.

"Well, then I look forward to meeting him."

Side by side they walked a little faster and chatted about Desma's future. Kallisto soaked in the sounds and the feelings silently. The sweet sound of her sister's happy voice and the sun on her face gave place for hope that the visitation she had encountered the night before was not set in stone. She had however, tossed the letters in the fire and written a new one to her child. She was told it would be a boy. She wanted desperately to confide in Desma, but she was only thirteen and had not experienced the world in the same way that Kallisto had. She may not take the news joyfully. Kallisto was a bit confused in her feelings. On one hand meeting this new god was a delight and on the other dying was frightening. Focusing on this moment was best.

Every tapestry called out to discover it's beauty. Every fruit demanded a taste. The marketplace was especially lively that day. Bartering commenced loudly and the smells of fresh baked goods offered a welcome distraction from what was to be a difficult night.

"Joseph!" Kallisto lit up like the moon on a dark night, "I knew you would be here." A tall slender old man appeared from behind a stunning tapestry. Desma took careful note of his grand motions and his mellow deep voice. He exuded joy, unlike her father, a gruff and dirty man. He put in long hours in the fields with the pigs and came home with the distinct attitude that it was the last place in the world he wanted to be.

"Kallisto, my dear! Who is this lovely child beside you?" His smile was warmer than the sun.

"Joseph, this is my sister, Desma. She is here to help me pick out everything I will need for this child coming soon." She revealed her enlarged abdomen with a smile.

"Desma, this is Joseph, the man that sold me the mirror," she had told her so much more already that this introduction was merely a formality to Desma.

The two nodded toward each other, smiled and in unison said, "So good to meet you." Joseph added, a note of pleasure in his voice at being honored to meet Kallisto's lovely sister.

"Joseph, we are in search of our final item. I have praised your wares all day and hope that you will have what I am looking for." Kallisto smiled playfully tilting her head as she spoke. "I would like a cradle."

"Ahh! Praise Adonai! He looks after all our needs," he raised his hands and continued, "a friend of mine who makes many of these beautiful pieces gave his son his first commission. Though he is not yet bar mitzvah*, he has been accepted as one who will have his first reading at synagogue a few months early. His knowledge of Torah is outstanding, and his skill is beyond his years. Adonai has granted him superb talent. He entrusted me with this exquisite cradle saying to me that someone special would be looking for it." Joseph went back behind the tapestry again as he spoke.

The girls whispered together laughing at the delightful nuances of old Joseph. Desma was impressed with his wares and told Kallisto that she now understood why this was her safe place. "There is a calming presence about him even when he is loud."

Joseph returned with a cradle that was far more than Kallisto had imagined. "Now, my child, he told me to take whatever you have to offer since it is his debut piece, and it has been made for you specifically. He said the one who asks for it was meant to have it." The light color of the wood the etched grape vines along with the bear carved into the end of it brought tears to her eyes as she ran her hand over each design. She considered the small boy to be laid in it staring at the bear and wondering about her.

"Joseph, it is exquisite! And the bear! Oh, how could he have known?"

"I don't know my dear girl, but it is most definitely meant for you."

"How old is this young carpenter?" She asked without taking her eyes off the workmanship.

"He is twelve."

"Twelve?" Desma burst out, "I am thirteen and I could not even imagine doing anything this creative and perfect." She tenderly stroked the wood and the etchings.

The money had hardly been exchanged when Kallisto grabbed her stomach in tremendous pain and gasped, "Oh! Desma! We must go. The baby will come soon."

"Girls, my son Titus will follow behind carrying the cradle for you. My prayers will go up for you, Kallisto." He hurried over to the other end of the tables and handed a handsome young man the cradle and shouted instructions after him as he pushed him toward the girls. He then started talking to the gathering crowd of curious shoppers.

Passing the temple of Artemis, Aphrodesia noticed the girls and rushed out to inquire about the pain and fear in Kallisto's eyes. Her normal soft countenance had completely disappeared, but she knew exactly what to do.

"She insists that the baby is coming soon."

Desma could hardly get the words out, her breath was scarce, and fear gripped her as well. "Her time has not yet come," she whispered.

"I will get the iatrine*. Do you know what to do until we get there?" Desma nodded focusing only on her sister and Aphrodesia ran as swiftly as her sandaled feet would allow on the dusty street.

Once back to the house Titus gently placed the cradle near the door hoping it would be out of the way and left without saying a word.

"Desma," Kallisto groaned, "I burned all the letters and wrote one new one. The letter to my son is in a small box under my bed. Do not tell Plouton anything until the boy is older. Make sure he is taken care of. He will need a wet nurse for 3 years; I have hidden money under the bed as well. You will see where I have dug for the box." She then lay her head back and moaned with another great pain.

"Kallisto, don't talk like this you will give the letter and tell the stories yourself." Desma encouraged through tears running into her mouth.

"No, Desma, I had a dream last night. More like a vision I guess," she paused with the pain. As it eased, she spoke quickly trying to get everything out while the two were alone. "An angel of Adonai came to me and told me that my soul would be required of me today. In His mercy, Adonai will allow my son to live. I have given Him my soul and that of my son." Pain was increasing too fast.

"Adonai? Who is this Adonai?" Desma was confused, her head spun with thoughts of everything she had just been told and the possible future events staring her in the face.

"Please!" Kallisto screamed through the next wave of pain. "Promise me before the iatrine arrives." She reached for Desma with one hand and her constricting stomach with the other.

"Yes, of course, but who is Adonai and what does he have to do with your soul?"

Kallisto took a deep breath in through her nose and out through her mouth as her face twisted with pain. "Talk to Joseph. I don't know, I told the angel that this boy now belongs to Adonai if He will take care of him until the time comes for him to be on his own." Her wispy voice trailed off as she fell back on her bed weakened by the pain.

Aphrodesia and the iatrine arrived at that moment, seeing Kallisto so weak they rushed to her side already assessing the situation. "I have the birthing chair" the iatrine started, "but, she is already too weak for that." She paused and took out tools and cloths as she continued. "I warned her early on that the diseases and beatings she had endured were too much. She should have let me take the child. I could have saved her life." Removing the blanket covering her legs she shouted out orders. Aphrodesia went right to work but, Desma sat frozen in the moment realizing for the first time that her sister was about to die.

"There is a rupture, and the baby will need to be removed from the mother or it will also die. We have only a few minutes." She turned and saw Desma frozen and staring at the scene before her. "Girl!" She yelled, "get some clean water from the well and fresh cloths to wrap the baby… and hurry!" she said louder attempting to snap Desma into action.

Desma reached for the water vessel on the counter and saw the swaddling cloths she and Kallisto had prepared earlier that week. Tears welled up in her brown eyes and she ran as fast as she could to the well for water. "Oh! great Artemis, please do not be angry with Kallisto. I know you have the power to save her life. Please do not send her to the stars. Take that baby instead," she prayed as she ran.

Before entering the house, she heard the cry of a baby and intuitively knew her prayer would go unanswered. Hot tears streamed down her dusty face.

Aphrodesia handed Desma the baby to clean and swaddle. She took him and against every desire to throw him out the window she washed and wrapped him tightly.

"I will get someone here for the body as timely as possible." Desma heard the iatrine tell Aphrodesia.

"Katara ton theon,*" Desma whispered angrily at the ruddy skinned newborn. "You truly are cursed of the gods, and that Adonai can have you. I don't want you. I want my sister," she hissed at the sleeping baby. She sat silently crying with Kallisto's body wrapped in bloody blankets. She thought of every moment she had ever spent with her sister promising herself she'd never forget any of them. "I love you, Kallisto." She said aloud believing she was heard.

Chapter 3

It could have been a few minutes or a few hours, she was unaware of time passing. The plans. The laughing. The cooking. The shopping… "the shopping!" she finally shouted. "Joseph!" She would have to find Joseph. Women came to prepare the body and gave permission to Desma to find a wet nurse. She grabbed the baby and ran to the temple looking for Aphrodesia. "I don't know what to do." She admitted, "I need a wet nurse* and I don't know anyone. Can you help?"

"Yes," said Aphrodesia solemnly. "Kallisto already made arrangements." Desma looked confused so she continued. "Well, she knew the delivery would be difficult and was warned that her death was possible, so she made the arrangements last month. She was always so considerate." Desma just stared in disbelief and nodded.

She knew? Desma thought. Together they took the baby boy to the woman's home and promised she would return the next day with the necessities and the money. It was dark before she made it home, alone. Kallisto was gone, the bed stripped bare and stained with the blood of a deadly childbirth. Desma

The Demoniac

laid on the edge of the straw-filled mattress on the floor sobbing until sleep overtook her weary mind.

Chapter 4

The morning sun rose the same as every day before, but everything was different. Desma got up and cleaned herself and put on a clean peplos. She positioned herself as she had seen Kallisto do before the mirror. She brushed her long, straight black hair and wished she had the beauty of her sister.

"Why?" She spoke to the silent empty room. "Why Artemis? Why would you take her and leave me with that wretched child?" Her eyes searched the reflection of the room. Everything brought a recent memory of her sister preparing dinner or washing clothes and telling stories of her studies at the gymnasium. The two of them laughing and dancing to imaginary music. She stared at the intricate etchings framing the mirror, all telling the story of Zeus and Callisto. *'Maybe it was Hera'* she thought. *'Maybe she was again jealous of a beautiful Kallisto. She did say that one day she would join the stars of The Great Bear.'* That thought gave her a glimpse of comfort. She vowed to look to the constellation for a sign every night.

"I will name him Kataramenos for he is cursed," she declared to the mirror.

The Demoniac

Since taking the cradle, blankets, and clothes to the wet nurse she had not returned for a visit and would be leaving for home soon. *'Maybe he will have died before I have to pay more,'* she silently hoped. She took the longest way and stopped off at several shops at the marketplace to waste time. Passing a small shop, she noticed a rattle with a bear painted on it. "You must take care of him until the time comes for him to be on his own." She heard Kallisto's final words resonate in her thoughts. She had promised. Paying for the rattle she sped up her pace to see the cursed one and his wet nurse.

"Desma," Aspasia spoke softly as to not wake the baby she held in her arms. "the boy is doing well." She motioned with one hand for her to come closer. The room was undersized and dimly lit but tidy. "Have you chosen his name?" She looked down at the infant which had recently fallen to sleep at this stranger's breast.

Desma held out the rattle as she glared at the innocent sleeping baby. She noted his beauty; he resembled his mother even now. She wanted to hate him, she wanted him to die but, in this moment, she wanted to hold him and tell him all about his mother and the significance of the rattle. "Kataramenos," she weakly whispered.

"Cursed?" Aspasia translated, confused. "But why? He is healthy and calm and easy to tend."

"He took the life of my sister," Desma retorted hatefully. Aspasia nodded and lowered her eyes toward the contented, tender baby nestled in her arms.

"I have brought the money required to cover the next several months of care. I will be returning to my family's home near Gamala. I am to be married in a month and then will return to Kallisto's home. I will come again when I return." She saw the graciousness in Aspasia's eyes and felt sorrow for her own hatred.

"Do you want to hold him?"

"No, I will let him sleep." To her own surprise she reached down and stroked his soft black hair and was sure she saw him smile in his sleep. With that she turned and left.

Going back through the marketplace she searched for the illusive Joseph. She had not seen him before or after that fateful day. *'Who cares?'* she thought, *'just another god to be angry at.'* Her return home allowed only two weeks to finish the preparations for the wedding. Her mother was so excited about her first wedding to plan. Her father was glad that the spending was nearly over. "Flowers! Wine! Chairs!

Food! Music! Everything is so expensive!" He grumbled more than normal.

Telling her family about the death of Kallisto and the life of her son was as difficult as she expected. Though she practiced the conversation in her mind all the way home it was not easy. Her mother was distraught, and her father reasoned that the favor of the gods may come to an end.

Her parents negotiated the dowry by adding in the house in Gerasa in order that less money came out of their own pockets. This gave her mother the freedom to spend more on the wedding party itself. A well-educated man from a wealthy family was a dream come true for her parents and a home in the middle of the Decapolis was a dream come true for that man. Living in that place was going to be sad for Desma, reliving the months prior to that tragic night.

His appearance three days before the wedding gave Desma chills. He was only 26 so at least that was a good thing. Maybe he would understand her promise to Kallisto to care for Kataramenos until he was able to be on his own.

As the name Kastor indicated she expected to see a beaver face. Upon the arrival of two men, she heard a thunderous man like her father and that terrified her. The man before her had big teeth on top, his brown hair and matching mustache accentuated them all the more. Though correspondence with her parents had afforded him the opportunity to learn about her sister's dedication to the gods along with stories of her beauty and favor but, of Desma he knew little. All that was said of Desma was that she was strong enough to keep a home well, and that she was trained to be a loyal wife and mother.

She watched his face intently in hope that he would reveal his thoughts about her appearance. Kallisto told her that she would be able to know the sort of man he was by his eyes and his smile, she hoped this was true. Kastor looked on her and his eyes softened as his face lit up in a warm smile. It was the kind of smile that melted all her fears. He no longer looked repulsive but strong and safe. His eyes were very light brown with flecks of green, something she had not seen often. His thick brown hair was wavy, and she knew in that single moment that he was capable of a tender heart. Only time would tell if her initial assessment were true.

"So pleased to finally meet you, Desma. I had no idea how beautiful a wife I was getting." His voice was warm like a bath at the end of a long cold day. The loud thunderous noise she had heard at his arrival was not his.

The Demoniac

She smiled and said nothing, not wanting this memory to fade. His eyes were mesmerizing. She hoped his touch would be gentle as well, she was certain that the advice given by Kallisto would help.

She heard the obnoxious booming from behind her and turned to see who found it necessary to interrupt this perfect moment. "That is my father," Kastor spoke up with such a softness that her mind was once again at ease.

Chapter 5

Each day sped past like lightning; her mother had arranged everything in order to impress this wealthy family. The decorations were delicate and romantic. She was rushing around so much that each day ended with her sinking into her sleep mat immediately after evening meal. The groom's family remained at a local inn until the day of the ceremony.

The day went by in a flash. The colors, the voices, the music, dancing, wine and food, everything was a blur. The wedding night was not as frightening after talking with Kallisto. She took her advice to heart. Kastor was indeed pleased, and she was also able to enjoy the time they shared coming together and drifting off to sleep next to each other.

Chapter 6

Just before dawn, Desma joined her mother and sisters in cleaning up after the guests while Kastor said his good-byes to his family, and he joined Desma's family for a morning meal. "This is the best meal I have had in ages!" He paused before adding, "Aside from the glorious wedding feast we shared last night. The ladies of your house are exceptional cooks." He smiled and nodded at the man of the house as a way of complimenting him on his choice of a wife and ability to raise his daughters.

"When will you be leaving for Gerasa?" her father asked without acknowledging the compliment.

"At daybreak," Kastor stated with a note of sorrow in his voice. Her father simply rose and went out into the courtyard. Her mother however, stayed and spoke with the newlyweds about the trip and the wedding and anything they may need for the journey.

"It will be several days," she finished with a sigh. "Oh, to be young again." There was an unfamiliar note to her mother's voice and Desma considered for the first time that her mother may not want her to go so far. "My children are growing up so quickly,

Kallisto was given to the gods so young, and we didn't see her for years and now..." she wiped tears from her cheeks, "and now you, Desma, I will miss you." The sentiment caught Desma by surprise.

"Oh, I know that each day is filled with work and your father is quite demanding but, I..." again she wiped tears from her cheeks and chin. "I cherish our times together. I only hope that I taught you well enough. Being a wife and mother is tough." She stopped to blow her nose and dry her eyes. "I will miss my young lady."

"We prepared food for your journey." Zena blurted out trying to join in on this rare moment.

"Yes, we did," mother agreed, smiling through the tears. "Things that will keep well for days." Together the girls put the foods into a leather sack along with the wine skins for water. "Kastor, there are several wells between here and Gerasa, make sure you stop at each one."

"Yes, of course, I will take good care of Desma."

The walk to Gerasa was both a sad and joyous event. The two talked about everything and when the timing felt right Desma explained her promise to Kallisto. She made a brilliant case to raise her sister's son. Kastor became silent as he considered all that would entail. "Well, we have over two years to make a life together and when the time comes, we will know the best path to take."

Returning to Gerasa was a disheartening time for Desma, even though Kastor was quite taken aback by the grandeur of the city. The first night in Kallisto's home, brought with it nightmares and little sleep for Desma. The next morning a young man entered and spoke with authority.

"This home was given to my master's woman and it has come to his attention that she is gone. You are not welcome here and must leave. He has sent me to prepare for another to live here." Without another word he turned and walked out the door leaving the newly married couple shocked and homeless.

Desma looked at Kastor fearfully realizing that this was a large part of the dowry and he had the right to call off the marriage. As suddenly as that thought came, every memory of the time spent there with her beloved sister flooded her memory and she was devastated at the realization that every memory would be left here and never relived; gone forever. Tears flowed down her cheeks and off her chin. She hid her face in her hands and sobbed uncontrollably. Kastor felt inadequate, and unable to help his bride. She finally slept, drained from extreme emotion.

Chapter 7

Morning sun rose like any other day and again she knew that it was not like any other day. A deep and long discussion during the preparation and eating of a morning meal determined their fate. Everything remained on the cart and unpacking was not an option. While attempting to pack Kallisto's belongings the servant returned with the demand that everything be left as it was.

"These items belonged to my sister and I will take them!" Desma shouted.

"Every item in this house was purchased with money given as a gift to my master's hetaera. You do not have any right to take anything." The young man stood strong on the side of his master and continued, "If you do not choose to obey his command to leave all of his things in this house and depart, he will have you thrown into prison as the thieves you are." He glared harshly into her eyes and left in the same manner as the day before.

Again, Desma wept bitterly. "My sister, my house, my family, my life, everything stolen from me." She was inconsolable and Kastor again was saddened by his inability to do anything. He left without a word, walking to clear his head and make plans.

Gedara was not too much further and with the money given to them at the wedding and the remainder of the dowry they would be able to find a place to live. He reasoned that the area right outside of town would be dangerous and Gedara was closer to the sea, bringing in many visitors willing to purchase his art. He could get a position right away as a money handler with a wealthy merchant with the degree he had. He returned to comfort Desma only to find an empty house.

She had gone to see Aspasia and Kataramenos. She took money to cover an additional two years and instructions in case she did not return when he turned three, she was to take him to the temple. She felt that this was the best thing for him. Kallisto never told her anything bad about the temple. There was no clear future for her and no guarantee that she would be able to care for herself let alone a child. She did give him a hug and told him to always look up. He was only three months old but maybe somehow, he would understand it. Aspasia was sorry for her and promised to do as she was instructed.

All the way back to the house she rehearsed her speech. She would explain that she would work hard to be a good wife and give him sons. She would promise to take work from anywhere she could in order to make up for the lost dowry. She knew the possibility was that Kastor would send her away. She recalled the overwhelming feelings of love and concern in her heart for Kataramenos when she looked at his sweet face; the longing to hold him just once. He snuggled down into her arms and she saw a smile cross his tiny pink lips. She kissed his forehead and handed him back. It didn't take long to explain the situation and excuse herself from Aspasia. The walk back to Kallisto's home was lonely and frightening. *Why did Kastor leave? Was he so angry that he couldn't think of what to say? Maybe he needed to find out how to divorce her because of a breach of contract.* She cried silently and slowed her pace.

She had kissed that soft cheek one more time knowing it would be the last time. If she were able to talk Kastor into keeping her she knew that raising that boy would be too much to ask. Aspasia also knew deep down that she would never see Desma again.

Chapter 8

Time flew by as it most often seems to do and Kataramenos went from snuggling into her breast for nourishment to crawling, teething and walking. By the time he turned 3 he was getting into everything and laughing as he ran away. He had been weaned for nearly 3 months, but no word had come from Desma since that day. Aspasia had no means to raise another child. She had 4 other children and her husband wanted nothing to do with raising the orphan. She had promised him that on his 3rd birthday she would take him to the temple of Artemis and drop him off. That was more favorable than just putting him out into the street since she had developed a deep love for him.

"We will be going on an adventure today," she told him as he dressed.

"Where?" came his precious little voice.

She helped him with his sandals and brushed his hair from his face.

"We are going to the temple of Artemis." She replied with as much excitement as she could muster. He smiled. She had told him many stories of Artemis and her love for children.

Together they walked through the streets and past the marketplace vendors. Kataramenos was distracted easily by the noise of the buyers and sellers shouting at each other before settling on a price. He saw the beautiful materials and fresh fruits, and smelled the food being cooked. Everything vied for his attention. As they left the marketplace he danced to the music until it disappeared. All the while Aspasia held his dirty hand and smiled with tenderness at this very active boy. He was so beautiful many people mistook him for a girl.

No one knows all that is required of the children offered to Artemis, but she reasoned to herself that it had to be better than the streets.

Aphrodesia met them outside of the temple, "he looks so much like his mother." She said with surprise. "I could almost think he was a girl."

"Many people say that. His mother must have been very beautiful."

"She was. And a dear friend."

"Well, Aphrodesia, Desma has never returned for him, he is now 3 and my husband refuses to raise another man's son. I have no way of knowing where she went so, I brought him to the temple to stay as I swore to do." Light reflected from the deep brown eyes filled with tears as she looked down at him and Kataramenos did not like that she was crying.

"Why you cry?" He said as he reached toward her tanned face. He swept a long black hair from her cheek and added, "I love you." She forced a smile where tears demanded to fall.

Aphrodesia took him and spoke gently to them both, "Well, Artemis is especially fond of strong beautiful boys and we have a place for you Kataramenos."

His forehead furrowed and his dark brown eyebrows scrunched to nearly one as he contemplated just what all this meant. Aspasia took his tiny face into her hands and held it, just watching his expression before kissing his cheek and saying, "I love you too Katara, and I am terribly sorry." She turned quickly before he could see the tears stream down her face and ran toward home. She stopped several times to cry. It was the hardest thing she had ever done.

Kataramenos screamed and cried for hours until he finally fell asleep alone in a room. Neither food nor water were accepted by him. His heart was crushed, and fear overwhelmed his thoughts. He called for

The Demoniac

Aspasia only to hear sounds of anger outside his door.

The next morning, he woke and realized just how alone he was. There was no one to help him get dressed and no clothes in which to dress. The food that had been offered the night before was gone and only a small cup of water was there on the box beside his mat. His precious cradle was long gone and the sounds of brothers and sisters no more. A chill ran through him and tears began again. The room was stark and cold with only a large mat and a wooden box. The window was up too high to see out. He wiped his nose and mouth with the back of his hand and tried to call out to anyone who would listen.

Aphrodesia entered with warm bread, fresh milk, goat cheese and figs. She smiled as he took the milk and drank. "Good morning, Kataramenos."

She spoke kindly.

He watched her as he ate in silence, his cheeks streaked with hours of unattended sorrow. Continuing to breathe deeply to make up for those hours and his inability to catch his breath between deep sobs, he pondered the sincerity of this woman with warm food and fresh milk.

The Demoniac

"I am called Aphrodesia, and I will be taking care of you for now. I heard Aspasia call you Katara, would you prefer that?" He nodded as he gulped down the bread. We will be teaching you here for a while about what will be expected of you later. There will be chores to keep you busy." She didn't offer a hug or even wipe his tears, but at least she didn't make him cry more. He finished the cheese and milk and grabbed for the figs as she lifted the tray and glass to leave him in solitude once again. The bitter silence ate into his bones and he curled up on his mat slipping away into mental darkness.

Chapter 9

Two days of staring at stone walls seeing shadows move and listening in the stillness to the indistinguishable whispers, Katara didn't move except for the meager moments with Aphrodesia and food. Fear remained on him like a heavy cloak and Katara was unsure of ever saying another word.

On the third day Aphrodesia entered with extra fruit as a treat and opened the wooden box beside him removing a clean chiton*. She gently wiped his dirty face for the first time. "Good morning, Katara," her voice invitingly warm and calm. "Today I will introduce you to the other children who have been here for a while. They all began their studies and training. Maybe you can find a companion."

The juicy fruit tasted so sweet, and the warm cloth over his naked body helped him feel a little better, yet his voice was absent. The chiton was soft, and he realized there was no itching from his new clothes.

The labyrinthine halls of the temple frightened Katara as he realized he wouldn't be able to find his way back. Then they entered a large room filled with other children sitting in chairs facing a large statue of a woman. He sat in awe as he listened to the stories the woman standing in front of them told. They were stories of Zeus and Hera, he remembered them from Aspasia. He tried to smile but his face was fixed in a stare.

"This is Artemis" the woman said as she touched the great statue. "This is her temple. We will be showing you what it means to serve her. Some of you will remain here and some will only be trained here to go to serve in other temples. Don't be afraid, you will be well prepared for whatever service you will do". All of the children looked around. Katara noticed they all wore the same chiton he was wearing. Some had longer hair and some were a little taller but for the most part they all looked the same.

Time crept by and finally several big girls brought trays of warm bread and cheese along with fruit and fish. Everything looked and smelled so good. Katara wanted to jump up and run to the table but the woman up front spoke loudly and demanded his attention.

"Children, we first dedicate ourselves, our actions, our thoughts and our food to the beautiful and powerful Artemis." She moved over to the table and stared at the statue as she spoke.

"Artemis, I give this food to you first. Use it to fill us and help us to honor you. I dedicate every child here to be used by you however you choose that they may prove greatness. Fill them with understanding of what an honor it is to serve you. Give me the words and actions it takes to teach them about you and your family, so that they may do well in any temple for any god. Show me where you want them to go. You love children so these children are now all yours". She then paused and looked at the twelve children in the room.

"You all may come now to eat and get your fill."

The other children laughed and spoke as they ate, but Katara sat alone in the midst of them absorbing every sight. The interesting large white stone with the black swirls running through it creating a huge statue of Artemis felt cold even from across the room. This was not a real person, but the woman spoke like it was. He wanted to touch it even though it was scary. Her eyes were not clear and had no color. He had grown up with a small statue of her but this big one was different. He took note of the other statues and scrolls opposite the side of the room from which all the children sat eating.

He felt very small as he looked around. The others were older but not by much and the women looked very tall. The peplos they all wore matched the statue. The bow Artemis held and the arrows in the quiver on her back caught his gaze. Her head was turned toward the far wall where a deer was painted. In the corner behind her was a small bear carved from a tree. Katara was sure it was real, and he knew that it would be dangerous to go near it. The smell of fish, olives, and apricots permeated the room. The flavors were delightful and Katara fully enjoyed the luxurious meal. He had grown up eating cheese, breads, grains and soup. Olives and fish were saved for special occasions. He thought of Aspasia and her beautiful eyes that lit up when she smiled. He had never seen her cry until she dropped him off here. *Why did she leave him?* He couldn't think of anything he had done that would cause her to hate him so, he always tried to be a good boy. *Although,* he thought, *I did spill that container of salt on the floor, and in the olives. Maybe that is why.* He began to cry and hid his face so the others could not see. *I'm sorry!!!* He screamed inside his head, even though she couldn't hear his thoughts so far from her house. She did have a way of doing so when they were close. He remembered dropping his bear toy in the mud and trying to hide it behind his back and she looked him right in the eye and asked. "Now, Katara, did you get bear-bear all dirty?" How could she have known unless she read his thoughts or could see right through him? Since you can't see through a person, she must have read his mind. That explained how she always found his hiding spots even if he hid behind the door or under the table, so he called out to her as loud as he could in his mind hoping that she would hear his sincerity and sorrow and return for him.

After lunch all the boys were told the story of the bear, which is now the Great Bear, Calisto, in the night sky. He thought again of bear-bear and the story Aspasia told him of his mother, "she is now among the stars in the constellation The Great Bear, watching over you." It was hard to understand, but it must be true because he had heard that story many times and now this lady was telling the story of Artemis and the bear.

"The girls are preparing to go to Brauron for the dance of the bear. You boys will be taking over all the chores so pay close attention as we show you everything that must be done and exactly how they must be accomplished. You will be expected to complete everything you are told to do with no discussion, and you will be required to honor our goddess Artemis. She does not take kindly to children misbehaving. Remember the story of the bear as we teach more in the coming days." The tall angry looking woman told them. "For now, this half of the room will follow Petron to the clothing room." She swooped her hand away from Katara, "and this half of the room will go with Kornos to the kitchen."

Katara quickly counted 5 going to the clothing room and 6 going with him to the kitchen. He had learned to count with Aspasia's older children. Numbers came easy however letters were not so easy.

The kitchen was a busy place with 8 big girls and 2 ladies rushing all around. Two girls washed dishes, two were cutting fruit and three girls were taking nuts from their shells while one girl was in the corner by herself washing the wall.

"What is your name?" He looked straight up into the face of the tall angry woman staring down at him.

"Katara," he whispered.

"Speak up!" she snapped at him.

"Katara," he said slightly louder.

"Well, cursed one, you will wash floors and walls for today. Go over there with that one." She pointed toward the lone girl in the corner and went on to the next boy in line.

Cursed one? I said Katara, maybe she can't hear well he thought as he neared the very sad little girl scrubbing as hard as she could. He took a rag from the bucket next to her allowing water to drain off into a puddle on the floor and running quickly toward the bottom shelf.

The Demoniac

"You made a mess! Now clean it up! I will not tolerate children playing or making messes!" the tall slender angry woman glared as she spoke.

To end the day another woman took the boys to a room full of beds and Katara was assigned one in the front corner near the door. The window was larger, so more light filled the room than where he had been before, but the boys could not see outside well since it was near the top of the wall. Periodically they saw feet pass by. Conversations were had, conjectures of the people passing. Most of the boys were only seven or eight and the older boys were no more than 10. They enjoyed imagining where they were located in the temple and why the feet were more frequent in the morning and in the late afternoon. Often the older boys would climb on the beds and stretch to see the young men headed for the gymnasium and the arena for competitions. The conversations were competitive in that they all decided which competition they would be best at if they were at the arena.

Katara was lonely as his roommates talked and played leaving him out of every conversation. He was only three and they believed he could not understand. He did understand more than they knew.

Chapter 10

As the dark closed in on the room the stillness was disrupted by moving shadows. Katara had not seen the door open, but he definitely heard a strange laughing sound that frightened him. He squirmed further into his bed till he was in the middle under his blanket and covered his ears with his hands. He hid as best he could by squeezing his eyes closed tightly. In his head he hummed a song Aspasia had taught him when he had trouble sleeping. It seemed like hours to his young mind before he fell asleep.

The next morning 3 of the boys were allowed to stay in their beds a while longer while all the others went to the room with the creepy statue and listened to more stories of the gods before eating lunch. Two of the boys joined them at lunch. At bedtime the last one was still in his bed. Katara was scared to enter that room with the terrifying laughter and mysterious dark shadows. He tried to explain to the lady in the work room, however the tall angry woman refused to try to understand his feeble attempt at explaining his fear. She unconcerned, so back he went with the others.

Each boy to their assigned bed. He was the smallest. Most nights played out the same as his first night there; eerie laughter coming from dark shadows escaping their prison of the stone walls. Accompanied by sobbing from different areas of the room, his fear was intensified daily. He was worn out from a lack of sleep.

All girls were taken to Brauron for the festival where they danced the bear with girls from all over the world. This was the reason the boys were required to take their place in the kitchen, thus eliminating the pre-lunch stories. Once in the kitchen the tall spiteful woman was replaced by a kinder looking lady. She was not as tall and didn't have any lines on her face. Katara took that as a good sign.

"Hello, I am Ophelia and I have been here at the temple for several years. I have helped just like you are doing now and have been placed in charge of all of you while the younger girls are away." She smiled and Katara's heart was eased. "These are our other helpers," she began looking around at girls that had entered the room behind the boys. "Helena, Melba, Delphine, and Zena," she pointed at the girls as she called their names and they waved. These helpers were older than he yet younger than 'the mean one' (as he called her). This was why he determined that he could trust them. The work went by easier and faster; nothing had changed in the process, but the heavy growly glares of 'the mean one' were not present.

The Demoniac

Great busyness distracted everyone and several but not all of the girls returned along with another new woman that entered and studied the size and looks of each of the boys. Katara sat silently studying her. A young man whispered things in her ear and pointed at several of the boys and each of them were told to leave with them. Every remaining boy was filled with confusion as to why they were not chosen.

That night was the first quiet night he could remember since being moved to the great room. He wasn't sure exactly why, but he figured it was that he must be the only one that had heard the others crying and had seen the spooky shadows. Before too long he had supposed that the boys chosen had been playing a trick on him.

Months passed before it all began again; the terrifying shadows moved around the room in the dark slowly, leaving crying roommates in their wake. At times he heard what he believed to be a scream that was abruptly hushed allowing a cold whimper to continue throughout the night.

The cries were closer this time and Katara wriggled down to the center of his bed and covered his ears with his hands and hid his whole body with his blanket. Summer was upon the land and the extra warmth of a blanket should have been unnecessary, but it was his only protection; it made him invisible.

The Demoniac

Time crept by and exhaustion overtook the boys. Twelve weeks had gone by and the same woman and young men entered the classroom picking their favorites and taking them away. This time new boys entered to take their place. Katara was the singular one left from the original group in the great room. He was devastated that he had been left behind to endure that horrifying room.

It must've been because he was smaller than the other boys, but he would soon be four and maybe then he would be chosen.

The stillness at night was a welcome change, he needed the sleep and deep down inside he knew it would be temporary. The days however were not any easier. The mean one hated him, and he could not figure out why. He was too afraid to ask.

Still nights were short lived. With the dawn he listened as the older boys discussed the reasons for their tears. Katara was glad for his size and that he could become invisible. He lay perfectly still as they told of the pain as the dark shadows hurt their penises and their butts and whispered terrible things to them.

"Did he visit you?" One of the oldest boys asked his friend.

"Not last night, but a few days ago he did." The second voice was familiar. Katara didn't dare roll over to get a look at them.

"He said I would be taken soon to serve the gods as a scapegoat. I was to bear the shame of everyone and that it was my fault anyway." The first voice said. "What does that mean?"

Katara strained to listen but no one said anything. He could keep quiet no longer and sat up to tell them about the man and woman that came to class and took boys away. He told them about the secret he had kept for nearly a year, about the scary shadows and fiendish laughter as the other boys had also cried at night. Eyes wide, each boy listened intently.

"Where do you suppose they are taken?" Hector asked in a shaky voice. He had been the first voice Katara heard. Everyone shook their heads and looked at Katara. "I don't know" he said with a shrug, "All I know is each time boys leave, the laughing stops for at least three weeks."

Myron had been one of the boys crying in the dark as was indicated by his still red face and the red spots around his eyes and cheeks. Niko asked him if he had been visited last night and he nodded and cried again. Niko was not much larger than Katara. "How old are you?" Myron asked Niko and watched as the child held up 6 fingers. "Did he hurt you?" He nodded but added that not the same way the others had said they were tortured.

"I was told," he began fearfully, "that I would be among the favored ones soon enough." I was not sure what that meant, and I don't want to know." Niko added.

Hector went around the room and found that the boys that had been crying were all 7. Katara held up 3 fingers quickly adding that he would soon turn 4 giving him more credibility. He noted that there were 3 empty beds, and he was three and there were 7 empty beds, and the other boys were all 7 except Hector who was five.

It was five days later when five boys came to fill empty beds. Numbers were so fascinating to Katara.

Chapter 11

Days always began the same, stories in front of the creepy stone statue, wood bear and painted walls before lunch then work. The work was different yet the same, whether in the kitchen or outside the boys always cleaned something. Outside days were best. The gymnasium was near enough that they could watch the athletes train for the Olympics. Excitement grew in each boy as they dreamed of one day taking lessons at the enormous gymnasium and then training. Running, jumping, throwing javelins and shot put along with chariot races were the talk of every evening. Events were discussed in such a manner as to imagine they were the actual contenders preparing for their eventual participation.

Thynomenos, (The mean one had finally given her name in his presence), brought all their dreams to a screeching halt when she announced that "ones such as they would not ever be allowed to be considered for the games to honor Zeus."

"Why?" Ten voices sounded as one.

Her sole response was that someday they would understand and then she laughed, an eerie and familiar laugh as she left the room. Everyone, except

The Demoniac

Katara, burst into discussion about how she was wrong and mean. Katara shrank into his seat as a cold chill ran throughout his body.

That laugh, he thought, *is the same laugh that I hear at night. Should I tell the other boys?* He pondered those thoughts for days before being awakened to her freakish laugh followed by the older 3 boys crying.

Chapter 12

Morning came and went and no one acknowledged Katara's birthday. Nothing was said about him being at the temple for 2 years. The only thing holding anyone's attention were the games happening in only a few months.

The same boys had been together for over a year now and friendships had formed. Katara and Niko were very dear friends even though Thynomenos told them they had no chance at being involved in the games the two played together as competitors in the long jump and many a race.

Older boys had settled into a no-joy existence. The night cries had stopped, and no one spoke of the cause. There was never a reason to celebrate in the temple, it was a life filled with work for both boys and girls.

New children arrived periodically, but there was an influx annually following the dance of the bear. Girls were given to Artemis from families with promises of her favor on the home. Aria joined the workforce 8 days before and Katara could not take his mind off of her lovely green eyes and black hair. She had put it into a braid with a ribbon in it and it flowed down her back like liquid ebony. He had never seen green eyes before. They danced when she spoke in her soft, kind voice. There had never been a more beautiful creature born to the world, of that, he was sure.

Today they were assigned to the outside cleanup together. He wanted to talk to her so that he could hear her response but, could think of nothing to say. He worked hard to impress her. After the first half of the day when being called in to take part in second meal she finally spoke.

"Do you like it here?"

"No." was all he could force out of his mouth. His brain responded with all sorts of reasons why he didn't like it here, but his mouth would not say any of them.

"Oh." Aria was stunned at his lack of conversation for the entire morning and believed that he must not like her even though she was certain she had done nothing to cause his distaste for her. She really wanted him to like her since he was so handsome. Then again, she was the outcast of her family. They had sent her here because of her wretched green eyes. What shame she had brought on her family because of her eyes. Everyone stared at her, except Katara who would not look at her nor would he speak to her. She must be hideous. She could never be married if no one would see past her outer flaws. Tears formed as the two slowly made their way back into the temple dining/classroom.

"Why do you cry?" Came a concerned voice from beside her.

"I wish I could be beautiful like the other girls. I was sent here for the shame I caused my family." She said slightly above a whisper as she sniffled back her tears. She wiped a dirty hand across her face and picked up her speed.

Katara sped up as well in order to keep next to her. "But you are the most beautiful girl I have ever seen. How could you say such things?"

She stopped and looked directly into his eyes. She had been taught that you could tell a lot from people's eyes. They are the window to the soul, someone told her long ago. Of course, that was because her father was letting her know at that moment that she was obviously defective and had no soul since her eyes were so light and such a disgraceful shade. His eyes were tender and honest. She began to walk again, slower so that she would not lose this boy. A smile crept across her face as she rehearsed his words in her mind.

The Demoniac

Second meal was finished and the two nearly raced outside, both hoping that the other would speak first. Katara could not hold everything in any longer. He wanted to tell her that she had consumed his every thought for the eight days she had been at the temple. That every night he was able to make plans for their future before going to sleep, allowing him to be able to rest for the first time in nearly three years.

"You really think I am pretty?" She questioned before he could determine exactly how to begin.

He stopped physically and mentally every motion and notion staring at her in unbelief.

"You did say that didn't you?" she asked with confusion.

"Of course," he began, coming to his senses. "You are the most exquisite girl I have ever seen. Your eyes are mesmerizing, and your hair is flowing ink that I could write a lifetime with. Your voice, soft and pleasant relaxes my mind each night so that I can sleep in a situation which is most difficult."

She melted. Tears bubbled into her eyes. She looked down so that he could not see her face. She picked up some garbage and wiped her eyes hoping to disguise the tears before turning those eyes back to him. She took a deep breath in through her nose and began, "You sure use big words. How do you know those things?"

"Well, I like words that are different; I listen to men coming from the gymnasium talking about their lessons. I imagine you and describe every lovely feature over and over before I go to sleep each night. I have made plans for our future."

He suddenly stopped, realizing that he may have just said too much. Looking at her he noticed a smile that lit his life.

Chapter 13

"Get up boys, today we will be setting out on an
adventure." Katara's mind immediately went back to
the day he turned three and Aspasia brought him
here to the temple and left without him. A chill ran
down his spine as he imagined this new adventure.
Ponos had been one of the wicked shadows that
entered the boy's room some nights. Katara was one
of the boys he especially liked. He told other
shadows that Katara was pretty and would be of
great value to Aphrodite.

His first encounter with Ponos was very
uncomfortable. He had been sleeping and woke to a
shadow slightly touching his boy parts. It didn't hurt
but it scared him that someone was doing that. He
couldn't see who it was in the heavy darkness. The
shadow moved from bed to bed. None of the boys
said a word but Katara knew they felt the same way.

At first there was only one; then others came. The
encounters became hate filled as words were
whispered in his ear while hands touched him
everywhere. He eventually felt the man's nakedness
next to him and within a short time the fingers that
had entered his butt were replaced by the shadow
man's own penis. Katara tried to scream but his

mouth had been stuffed with a cloth and a large hand covered his face leaving only his nose available to suck air between silent screams.

The next morning Katara and 3 other boys were excused from work and he finally understood the muffled cries he'd heard for almost 3 years.

Time had told the story and today Ponos' voice was no longer a whisper but a loud proud voice echoing of an adventure. Each boy looked at the others and fear was reflected in their eyes. They had all been told about their upcoming duties and requirements as they lay helpless and silenced in their beds at night.

"It will be a long trip but, I will personally accompany you all to your next assignment."

"To Cyprus. Aphrodite's temple has been sending word that there is a need for boys such as yourselves. We will leave as soon as breakfast is done. There is no need for you to take anything with you, so our load will be light."

Katara wanted to take his bear. The one given to him at birth from his aunt to remind him of his mother looking down from her place in The Great Bear and make her proud. It was small, so he hid it in his sleeve and told no one.

The Demoniac

Just as promised the group left together after breakfast. Ponos gave each boy a sack which held figs, bread, and cheese. They were informed that these would need to last until they arrived at the next temple. Once outside they were joined by several of the girls that worked in the kitchen.

Katara found comfort in knowing that Aria would be coming with them. She had not been at the temple for a long time. He always tried to work near her so that they could talk. Her green eyes exploded with joy as she told stories of her family and her dreams. One day she was telling him about a dream in which he was all grown up and was strong and powerful and everybody was afraid of him except her. She twirled her ebony locks as she spoke, and her smile comforted him. He hoped she would someday marry him. As they all walked together, he imagined the two of them as grown-ups making dinner together and laughing since her laugh made his heart soar. He knew that there was not another girl for him, Aria stole his heart and every other thought from day one.

After several days of walking the entire group boarded a ship. This really had turned out to be an adventure. The ship was magnificent! The sails almost touched the sky and Katara counted 28 people besides the 17 in his group walking around. The sea was bright as the sunlight bounced off every movement of the water.

Maybe, he and Aria would someday own a big boat and sail all over the place. The world now appeared much larger than he ever knew. He had heard stories of the men who traveled to Mount Olympus to compete in games to honor Zeus. That had been his dream until he was told that he would never be allowed.

Some girls were taken to Brauron to dance the bear and would return with wonderful tales of their journey and the vastness of the outside world.

There were also stories from new boys that were terrifying; parents making them walk between rows of fire and seeing other kids dropped into a fire from the arms of a statue of Molech. Those stories made everyone grateful for just being given to Aphrodite to work.

Ponos whispered about the temple children being used for the pleasure of men and the release of their guilt. He told them that their only hope was to be a hetaerae and gain the favor of a rich man. He would seal those secrets with his lessons about what to do and how to do it or what not to do; always painfully expressed.

On the ship Ponos was well liked. He talked and laughed and drank till late at night they took turns making the boys cry. Katara decided that the other men may not know about Ponos' secrets because he didn't want to believe that every man was as bad as him.

The last moments before leaving the boys at the glorious temple of Aphrodite he curled his lip and glared at Katara and said, "You will be the most favored of all who come here. The gods cursed you from birth and many will choose to pile on those curses and leave you more broken than any other." His fiendish laugh sealed hatred in Katara. Ponos slithered away like a demon as the children were escorted into the side entrance at the base of the temple.

The magnificence of the temple was awe inspiring. Standing beside the columns made Katara feel tiny and insignificant. He looked out across the sea to the horizon and realized the world was significantly larger than he had been able to imagine as a little boy. Now, that he was 6 and nearly all grown up he could comprehend so much more.

The trip was exhausting, and the children all slept in one large room on bed mats filled with fresh straw, giving them the luxury of sleeping as long as they liked. Once awake each child was taken to a large cold room of marble. The light entered from every direction and as beautiful as it was blinding. There were many people sitting on long cushioned chairs with only sheer tunics. It didn't bother any of them that they were only slightly less than naked.

Katara took a deep breath and stood taller as he straightened his back and tried his hardest not to stare. After all, he wasn't a child anymore and this was obviously the grown-up room. Men entered from the far right of where he had entered and would approach a person lounging and the two would leave together through a wide doorway leading down a well-lit corridor.

Venesius was talking quietly to the small group of children but they were fully distracted by the action going on around them. Periodically another child would join the group and by the time they exited the grandiose lounging room all 17 children had been reunited.

Hurrying, Venesius ushered the group toward a darker corridor in the back of the room. As they walked, she asked questions that no one was able to answer.

She was small and lovely. She had four braids joined together over top of her stunningly long black hair. Katara tried counting the beads in each braid but she constantly moved and turned to face the group and he would lose count. She had a kind smile and a soft angelic voice. Her chiton was light and flowed as she walked but it was not sheer, he noted. She also wore an epiblema* over her soft shoulders. Her eyes were the same green color as Aria's, and they also announced her unique beauty even before she spoke a word. All the boys were fixated on her form.

"And finally, girls, you will be staying here with other girls you may have met at the temple of Artemis, as well as some that may be new to you. We hope you will enjoy each other's company." Katara waved to Aria as they both entered a tremendous room filled with the same mats they had been privileged to sleep on the night before. "And boys you will stay over here across the hall and down a short way."

Seventeen steps, Katara thought, *to get to Aria each day.*

Venesius repeated to the boys what she had apparently been telling them all the way down the corridor. "Please remember that you will be punished for going into the girl's room or for not being quickly obedient when called upon to do any required duty of special temple boys."

Katara's hair stood up on his arms when he heard 'required duty of special temple boys.' Those were precisely the same words whispered to him in the darkness. He wanted to run and hide.

The Demoniac

Did this enchantress understand what that meant? Was she somehow a charmer used to lure the newcomers into situations of shame and pain without any remorse? How could he have been so blinded by her? Why did he allow himself to trust an adult just because of her soft tender voice and stunning green eyes?

"Stunning!" he declared aloud and everyone, including Venesius turned to look at him. *She stuns us with those eyes and then captures us like a jugularis snake, I must continue to look down,* he thought to himself as he entered the boy quarters, *so as to not get caught in the hypnotizing view of such a loathsome person as Venesius.*

After choosing beds and discussing the entirety of the journey the boys were met by Solarius, a young man that introduced himself as their personal guide. He told them his story of arriving on Cyprus about 10 years earlier. He was timid and afraid. He had been orphaned by the death of his parents in a raid on his small town and he was chosen to serve Aphrodite for which he said he was grateful.

"I understand that each of you have also been chosen to serve Aphrodite for the next 10 years or so. To start with, while serving Artemis you will be introduced to the type of positions you will be expected to fill. We will have other opportunities later in life but for now this is of utmost importance. As Venesius explained, Aphrodite is the goddess of love. Therefore, you will be expected to be whatever anyone asks you to be for them. This is a form of worship. We offer love, acceptance and forgiveness as they request.

Some days, especially in the first months here you will serve the other, more experienced temple boys. They will teach you, so be sure to use this time wisely in order to learn all you can from them. They will give you tips to make this less painful and allowing our clientele to awaken to their love. They will release all guilt, shame, fear, and at times anger into you. You will be the eromenos* and if you are so blessed, you will catch the eye of an erastes* and eventually become his private hetaeros until you are on your own."

The boys all sat motionless in silence with mouths and eyes opened wide.

It is a lot to take in but, remember to learn from those you will serve for the next several months. You will each be awarded a new chiton* as well as the one you are wearing, and food will be given twice daily. We eat very well here. He smiled. No one returned the gesture.

"Well, if any of you have questions, I will be pleased to answer them. I have been assigned to the room next to this one and am available at any time." He paused as if expecting someone to say something then turned and left them alone.

The young boys sat in silence contemplating all they had just been told. Some began to cry while others wandered around the room pretending to be concerned with their previous bed selection. No one spoke.

Solarius brought food that evening to a tense and detached group. He tried to engage them to no avail. He concluded that before long they would fit right in and explained that this life was not chosen but, most of the boys and young men were given this opportunity above death or street begging. With that he looked around the room and took a mental note of the prettier boys. He commented that some of them would be more active and more requested, but each would be readily blessed by the gods for their service. Again, he simply left and this time he was humming his own tune.

The boys looked around the room at each other without saying a word, taking note of those Solarius had nodded toward. Every boy took an extra-long look at Katara.

The Demoniac

Chapter 14

Food was tasty, and sleep was welcome. The following months were a blur. Washing tunics or dishes, sweeping floors and polishing tables along with the lessons from older temple boys. Many lessons played out in hushed angst making each one acutely aware of the situation in which they had been thrust.

Katara was taller than most 6, almost 7 year olds. No one asked his age or even his name after the first day. He was given a temple name, Kat. That would be the only name he was to offer or to which he was to respond.

Egyptians coming to the temple would often ask for him to wash their dusty, sweaty bodies since they worshiped cats. They would often express their delight in being cleansed by a magical child. Good fortune had been their guide and would certainly follow them. They often asked him to go before his gods as well to give them extra blessings for being cleansed in that temple. The bath house was annexed to the most prominent and glorious lounging room [as Kat called it]. The youngest boys were used as cleansers there before graduating from physical cleansers to spiritual cleansers.

The qualifications were based on size and experience rather than age and Kat was the first in his sleeping quarters to be reassigned.

He had not made friends since no one talked much anymore. The days were long and filled with things to do, none of which were either fun or exciting. Both Venesius and Solarius had dampened every ounce of delight upon their arrival.

Aria had been seen a few times from a distance over the last six months, but now Kat was moving into a new room, far away from everyone he knew.

The new room was large enough for a bed mat, thicker than the previous one, and a small chest with a pole attaching it to both the ground and the ceiling which captured Kat's imagination.

"Many have admired your beauty, Kat, and desire your presence for spiritual cleansing," Malleus said, "I will now be your spiritual guide. I will do my best to help you in your new position." He smiled in such a way that reminded Kat of Thynomenos. A cold chill ran down his spine and goose bumps formed on his arms raising every hair.

"Our lessons begin now." Fear enveloped Kat. He searched for any possible way of escape reluctantly concluding that he was trapped like a caged animal with no way out. The only window was too high to reach and was not able to be opened. Malleus was directly in front of the door and approaching slowly. His voice was a droning noise unintelligible to Kat's racing mind.

"The men here will tell you everything. You can choose to listen or find an escape in your mind." Kat focused on his lips as Malleus continued. "They will release every form of guilt, shame fear, angst and passion."

At seven years old Kat didn't fully grasp all that Malleus was telling him but, it all sounded very frightening. He was trapped in a small space with a strange man explaining something Kat didn't want to know and definitely didn't want to participate in.

"Most often they don't want you to say anything or make any sound at all. In order for you to be requested you will need to please them in every way. Let each one tell you what they want and then follow through with their demands."

Malleus stepped to the side and Kat imagined quickly running toward the locked door and escaping. He saw himself passing each hallway and column past the bath house and finally to the outside world. Malleus had stopped talking and watched Kat cautiously. He himself had been in this very same situation only 6 years earlier. He was small and had been the last one from his acquaintances to be transferred to this section of the temple. He knew the anxious thoughts Kat was filtering through his young mind.

"Kat," he began again softly, "there is no way out. You will be accompanied to the outer courts in a few days. The grounds on which we live are some of the most beautiful in all the world I'm told." He was seeing the anxiety subside in his newest young acolyte. "Seeing the world from atop this mountain is awe inspiring. The sun glistens on the marble causing one to believe the impossibility of a universal creator."

Kat's breathing slowed, and he gave in to the inevitability of his assignment. The actions and dark whispers of Ponos and the eerie laughter of Thynomenos had been a foreshadowing of future events. They told him about the poverty, starvation and slow death he had been spared. They whispered about the depravity in which others came and exposed him to. Their cleansing would be part of the filth and horrors that would be released inside him. The laughter that rang in his mind haunted his sleep as well as his waking hours. When given the position of physical cleanser he began to find comfort in believing that they were liars and only found pleasure in tormenting him. However, entering this room his thoughts were flooded with the words, touches and unwanted painful actions forced on him as well as the overwhelming panic as his mouth was filled and the hands covered his face. He could barely breathe as Ponos rammed himself inside Kat.

His breathing became increasingly labored, and his heart reacted frantically as those memories resurfaced. His muscles tensed as they recalled that pain once again. Malleus inched nearer watching closely, taking Kat into his arms to comfort his anxiety.

"It's ok to feel this way." He attempted to console him. "We all have been through this. The preparations you experienced were to be the hardest and most difficult you may encounter. I will show you the gentler side of things." Malleus held Kat tighter and felt his chest raise and lower as he sobbed.

"We are not the nobility of the world; alas, we are not the least of all either. There are some who will release all their animosity toward civilization and the gods that allow unexplainable atrocities. But there are many that come wanting a free expression of their passion to be accepted by another. Some choose the girls or one of the women doing her duty before marriage; then there are those that choose only the boys. Your delicate features will no doubt find you to be favored among those. If you will allow each one to experience pleasure your chances are higher to be purchased by a patrician as his own hetaeros. That would possibly allow you to leave here sooner."

There was a long pause as Kat calmed and reminded himself that he is now 7 and nearly grown. *Pretty soon I will no longer be required to obey anyone, and I will honor only myself,* he thought. *I will go far away. There has to be a place somewhere for a young man to live without worry. I will find that place and stay there.*

Malleus spoke gently as he sat down with Kat on his lap. "One way to get through it is to purpose inside you that it is pleasurable to you as well." He smiled, and Kat frowned. "How old are you Kat?"

"I am 7, almost a grown-up." Now, Malleus frowned.

"Haven't you been here for a while?"

"Yes, six months and twelve days." Malleus crinkled his forehead and tilted his head. "I like numbers, so I count everything." Kat explained. Malleus nodded.

"Well, you could count during each ritual. It may be just the thing to keep your mind off of what is happening."

"But that doesn't mean that it brings me pleasure." Kat pointed out.

"No," Malleus admitted, "but, it helps to escape sometimes in any way possible. One of my favorite things to do is imagine going out on to the portico of the temple and watching the sun set at the edge of the world." Malleus stared off as if he were observing that at this very moment. Kat tried but found it difficult since he had never actually seen such a sight. Malleus cleared his throat, refocusing to the here and now. "Sometimes I imagine being on a ship, sailing far away. I imagine the wind blowing my chiton and my hair free of coverings, flowing free." He breathed deep and began again, "Sometimes I even imagine having a wife near me on the ship. There has to be a place I can go where that is a possibility." He sighed and put his arms around Kat who wiggled a little before settling down into this exploration of imagination.

Malleus left Kat to his imagery to look for Solarius finally finding him in the barber shop. "He is barely 7 years old! Most boys are older than that when they arrive, and he has already been initiated." Malleus was clearly upset.

"Just do what you have been told. There are many that have specified their desire for him." Solarius paused, "Besides, he is as large as the others. You have only 10 days before we allow him to join the place of choosing, so take care to teach him or I will call up Theron. He is a much stronger teacher with no reserve. Is that your desire, Malleus?"

"No, he is my acolyte. I am very capable of this assignment, Solarius." He turned and left the barber shop. He went directly back to Kat's dimly lit room, lay next to him and whispered, "Our lessons start now."

Chapter 15

During Artemesian men and women came and went. The musical competitions allowed for a sweet oasis for Kat's mind to wander to. The athletic competitions brought life to the entire island. It was similar to the Olympics in a small way. Excitement for those few days was enough to last for weeks at mealtimes. Some of the girls spoke about the romances of singles coming to meet and even marry.

The older temple servants discussed the theater. People had come from all over the world to be a part of each of the events. Kat heard some of them talking about the money that had been brought to the temple. He had never known that the temple was such a place of wealth. Some women came and waited outside to find a suitable husband. Some came to pay their due to Aphrodesia before their wedding day. They were offered any amount and willingly took anyone to the special place.

All the commotion of those few days elevated the excitement for weeks. However, the summer heat came early and the sailors flooded the island that year. Men from the bath house splurged on fine wine and dining while watching the girls and women splash around enticing the drunken sailors into the special rooms. Kat was used as a bather and would frequently be required to allow these men to use him for their pleasure. Greek and Roman soldiers frequented the temple, becoming regulars for their favorite temple servants.

Everyone had told Kat from the beginning that his delicate features would bring him favor and so it was. He had hoped that favor meant that others would be nice to him and that he would be granted his freedom early. The exaggerated favor he experienced was actually not favor at all, in his opinion. Many told him that it was almost like being with a girl to be with him, yet they didn't feel any remorse for telling their wives they had not been with any other women.

Some would demand that he perform for them while others were in and out of his special room in a matter of minutes spewing all forms of bitter rage at him throughout the entire process.

Chapter 16

By the time the air had cooled with the new season Kat was very ill. A local physician came to check on him and prescribed rest. Commenting on his youthful voice, the physician asked his age and was told that he would soon be eight.

"You are very tall to be that young, but your voice does give you away. I will return shortly," he said leaving his leather bag full of physician tools by the bed on the small table with the pole attached.

"He is not yet of age to be used so prominently." Kat overheard the man tell Solarius not far down the corridor.

"Hectarian, we pay you to get them back to health as quickly as possible, not question our judgment."

"Yes, but the statutes of Aphrodite are to allow cleansing by anyone 8 and older and that they would first be used as physical cleansers for minimally 6 months prior to that. He has been worked nearly to death and he is not yet of age."

"Again, Hectarian, these subjects have been deemed suitable as temple cleansers for anyone wishing to gain their innocence and youthful beauty. For anyone to be here their family has either offered them to the gods or the streets. We feed them and clothe them and train them. They are ready when we say they are ready."

"Solarius, you recall the days of your youth, you were subject to such work." Solarius nodded without looking up. "I stepped in for you and you were already almost 10. The diseases already raging in that boy could kill him before he reaches 10. I beg of you, show him mercy,"

"I would have been chosen as a hetaeros* if I had his beauty and his size," he snarled, "but, I am not so blessed by the gods. Now at 17 I will be released with nowhere to go. I hate boys like him. The temple has taken in a great number of offerings in order to request that one. More than I have taken in for the last 2 years! Mercy? NO, I will allow the gods to take him first!"

"Solarius, he is unable to work for now. He lies close to death. I will return every three days until he is better. But he must be placed on the unavailable list for now or others will not be cleansed but damned."

With a great sigh from Solarius the conversation ended and Hectarian returned. His instructions were to stay in bed and rest. He left herbs to be used in hot water and food and wine for the stomach.

Kat nodded and closed his eyes. He was tormented with dreams filled with sailors and soldiers along with tourists coming to the temple to find love from Aphrodite. He was restless, and sleep was not welcome. The pain was terrifying both physically and mentally. No one came when he called out yet each morning and each evening someone left figs, olives, cheese and bread along with wine and warm water.

Unable to walk for any distance found him designating a certain corner for excrement and urine.

Malleus entered the room after 12 days; Kat noted the number of times he woke to food and drink and cut that number in half in order to keep track of time. He knew he must do this so that he could stay in his right mind. He had gathered from Solarius that no one cared about him at all and he wanted to be sure to know how long his sickness lasted.

"Kat, I only just learned of your illness," Malleus said kindly. "Solarius updated me on all of the temple boys this morning before being dismissed."

"Where is he going?" Kat queried.

"It is time to begin the preparations for Aphrodesia. As a celebration of the birth of Aphrodite many new people are accepted here at her temple and those who have been here for many celebrations are sent away. This will be his final celebration for Aphrodite. He has been here for 10 celebrations and will now be sent out as a man to begin his own individual journey of life. Good riddance I say. He was not an adequate representation of the love of Aphrodite."

"When will you leave?"

"I will remain until the next celebration of her birth."

Kat closed his eyes. *When will I leave here?* He thought. *What day is it? What year is it?* His mind was slow, but frantic. He had never lost track of numbers or dates before except that 10 days once before. This frightened him almost as much as the conversation regarding his health.

"Hectarian will be here in a day or 2 to check on you. There are others that are sick as well. We had many sick after the festival, but you have been the worst according to Solarius."

"How long have I been sick?" Kat's voice was weak, and he hurt to move.

The Demoniac

"You have been in this room for 22 days."

Kat's eyes grew big, and he turned his head quickly toward his guide. "I counted only 12 days." His head reeled, and his thoughts raced frantically.

"The physician gave you medicine to help you rest and you were able to take it at first but suddenly there was a negative reaction. And you almost died." Solarius said that he checked on you daily and removed unconsumed nutrition. Hectarian has come every 2 days. He was here this morning. I spoke with him after speaking with Solarius.

Kat apologized for using the corner of the room as a latrine but, Malleus shook his head and assured him everything was ok. "It is good that you are awake, but you need more rest. I will return at sunrise on the morrow."

Kat cried himself back to sleep. He had somehow lost 10 days again. He prided himself in the perfection of numbers, times and days. The medicine Malleus gave him before he left helped him sleep for a while. When he woke, he heard others crying and angry voices; He couldn't make out the words, but the voice was certainly Thynomenos. He curled into a ball on his side to make sure he disappeared into the darkness beyond the reach of a star's light through the window. Try as he may, sleep escaped him and freakish laughter from his youth taunted him until the sun awoke.

Hectarian came a day earlier at the request of Malleus. He touched Kat's head and stomach then checked under his tunic to make sure that he was no longer showing signs of infection. His back, rectum and thighs were all visibly perfect and except for the pain in his head and the spinning room, Kat felt fine.

"Two more days of rest and he will be ready for work." Hectarian told Malleus. "No more bruising on his back and everything else looks fine as well."

"Thanks to you," Malleus said as he walked with him outside the room and closed the door.

"What bruising on his back were you talking about?" Malleus asked.

"The beating he sustained was substantial. There was a most impressive amount of internal damage for sure."

"I knew nothing of a beating."

"Well, I was told that he fell out of bed while suffering with his illness, however I am well aware of the difference between a fall from a short distance and a beating." Hectarian raised his eyebrows and shook his head. "He was beaten nearly to death. As if the diseases were not enough. Solarius would not give any information as to who did it to him, so I will never know, but he was most assuredly beaten."

Several minutes slipped by with no sound before Malleus reentered the room. "Kat," he began, "do you know who hurt you?"

"No," he said. "I know I felt pain but, I remember very little. I thought I was only sick. I have lost 10 days." He wanted to tell his spiritual guide just how scared he was. He wanted to tell him about the angry voices and laughter during the night, and the crying but, he feared retaliation.

Malleus removed the herbs and medicines that Hectarian had left to help him heal and exited the room. Fear took hold of Kat instantly as he realized he could trust no one. Why had he taken the very things that would make him well? How could there be hatefulness and deceit in the temple of love? Was Malleus friend or foe? Why is Thynomenos here? Was she out to find him and was Ponos nearby? Each question led to another. Solitude and sleeplessness left Kat increasingly fearful. He tried to remember the beating Hectarian claimed he had endured.

The Demoniac

In the twilight, Kat saw a figure sitting by him and recollection kicked in. Solarius' furious eyes and the pain as his fist struck his stomach repeatedly. Immediately he gasped and rolled toward the wall aware of the truth. Malleus touched his arm gently and Kat screamed.

"It's me, Malleus." His heart sank for the boy. *I knew he was much too young to be used,* he thought. *This is still far more than I expected.*

Kat bolted straight up and hugged his guide. "It's true!" Tears rolled onto Malleus' shoulder. "Hectarian is correct. I was beaten by Solarius. He came in the night and forced himself inside me, beat my stomach until I threw up then shoved me onto the floor..." He paused as his mind searched the darkness. "He gave me tea to drink... lots of times... and then he told me things... terrible things," he spoke with exaggerated pauses and winced at the memories returning, "frightening things." His face morphed and he hissed out words.

Malleus listened in reticence, his demeanor also changing. "So, it was Solarius," he whispered, more to himself. "Don't worry; I will take care of this." Malleus left the room knowing there was nothing that could be done at this juncture. With Solarius being relocated to the festival of Aphrodesia and then his release to live anywhere, finding him would be nearly impossible. Malleus contemplated going to the location of the upcoming festival but, his request would surely be denied. Right away he took the herbs he had removed from the bed side box to a different in-house physician and inquired as to their effects. He was informed that these were intense sleeping herbs and would allow even the most anxious person to sleep. Only a tiny amount was necessary and if given too much said person would never wake.

"Could one sleep for days or be severely abused without their knowledge once given these herbs?" He tried piecing together the last several days as he questioned him.

"Yes, I suppose. The dose would be tricky since the passionflower and the catnip mixed with valerian can only be administered for a short time and in small amounts. I would recommend only one of those at a time. Where did you get this mixture?"

"It was given to an acolyte of mine. I am not sure how long they were used but, I believe it was malevolently done."

The physician shook his head and clicked his tongue. "What reasons were expressed for such a concoction?"

"He had become ill following the Artemesian Celebration* and was left in his room aided by an older spiritual cleanser to recover."

"This mixture is not advised for such an illness. It is for excitability or insomnia." The physician studied the herbs again as he continued. "They can, however, be purchased separately at any apothecary."

Malleus was put at ease realizing that Hectarian had not likely misused medicines on Kat. "Thank you," he nodded and rushed out into the long corridor. Entering the darkened room, he promptly opened the curtain allowing light to flood in and told Kat that he needed to get up and move around so that the herbs could wear off. Turning toward him, he saw a new look of terror.

Chapter 17

Kat growled and reached forward scratching the cheek of Malleus and drawing blood. "Kat, it's ok, it is me, Malleus." He reached for his bloody cheek and stared in awe at his young acolyte. The sting of the scratch was nothing compared to the pain of an awareness of a horrible change in the boy before him. Tears welled up in his eyes as he turned to leave the room, closing the door behind him as much to protect Kat as it was to protect everyone else.

In that moment everything changed. Kat never allowed Malleus to be close to him emotionally again. Malleus found it difficult to guide him. His regulars rapidly requested other kedeshah*.

Kat formulated a plan to escape each day becoming more secluded in order to keep his plan a secret. Fear and anger combined to create an entirely new personality within him. Light, even from the moon would hurt his eyes and over the following months he was called on by only one man.

Plouton came to the temple only during the Artemesian Celebration. He had been the first to request young Kat to be his spiritual cleanser as well as his physical cleanser. He was a mean man that required silence as he performed several specific rituals, all of which were fiercely painful.

Kat remembered every detail and became submissive in order to reduce the pain. The second Plouton exited the special room, Kat cried and screamed out. His back was so sore he could not walk and the pulling of his hair had caused immense pain in his head. The other pains had become the norm.

Hours passed before anyone else entered the cold, dark room. Pulling back the curtain, Malleus discovered torn flesh on his back and a bed soaked with a tear-blood combination. His repeated apologies fell on deaf ears. Kat remained still as a statue and his heart had hardened exponentially toward everyone. Malleus dared not touch him but, swore to have the temple physician check on him. He set food on a small wooden table next to the pole. Shortly thereafter a doctor accompanied his guide back into the room. Evening had come making the wounds difficult to see.

The candle used to see dripped carelessly onto an open wound and Kat rose in ferocious rage lashing out at the one causing more agony. Instead, he again hurt Malleus who left, sobbing. The physician attempted to calm him, still not realizing that the wax had caused this outrageous show of savage behavior.

The Demoniac

"I cannot, nor will I attempt to aid you in your healing unless you calm down and act as a kindly young man," the stranger declared.

Kat couldn't care less if this was supposed to aid him in his healing he would just as soon die. "I will return in the morning and you will be sedated, or I will leave you to suffer!" Before leaving he laid a small herb on the table near some water.

Kat was indeed suffering; however, he had been tricked before and he'd lost memory of 10 days. In time he had remembered the cruel handiwork of Solarius and the panic that now plagued him. He terrorized people that entered his special room if they caused him any concern. Somehow, he yielded himself to the man who always demanded silence yet found himself to be in a worse predicament than before. His only consolation was that the memories of those lost days summoned to the surface were broken. This was fresh and complete. The pain, the agony and the fury released into and on him was as tangible as if a living force infiltrated his very being and merged with something vicious and massive.

The Demoniac

Chapter 18

Every day became a darker abyss to his mind. Men and women entered his room; Kat focused only on leaving. Escape plans formulated and reformulated. He ate very little and worked hard to bulk up his torso and arms. Power encompassed every thought. Power to cleanse. Power to choose life or death for each person that approached him. He fought the desire to kill another human, although the temptation increased with each passing day.

Chapter 19

The Olympics were once again taking place at the end of the hot months and this was his chance. As a 10-year-old, he was the size of the other 14 year old young men. He had the maturity of a mid-teen as well. The island was overrun with visitors from all over the world, paying homage to the gods.

The man who demanded silence had visited twice a year and would only accept Kat as his cleanser both physically and spiritually. His obsession confounded all of the older guides. Kat no longer withdrew, but welcomed the opportunity to become one with this entity. Each encounter replenished his inner evil. The man had informed Kat that he would stay in Cyprus for an extended period to celebrate Aphrodesia as well as gaze on the Olympians. Their union manifested an unfathomable malevolence in Plouton as well. His harsh gravelly voice created abominable scenes played out in Kat's mind.

When Plouton petitioned Aphrodite for Kat's accompaniment to the games her priestess very quickly agreed, feeling as though this had been the answer to her prayers.

The two left the temple together and stopped to admire the stunning beauty of the sunrise from the portico on top of the world. "Surely this is the home of the gods for no other place in the world is as breathtaking." Plouton spoke to Kat in a surprisingly unexceptional tone. His eyes were dark but gentle here in the light of the morning. This was a side of him that Kat assumed was nonexistent. He stared at the man beside him without a word for several seconds before taking in the wonder of this sight.

Freedom! So, this is freedom. Kat thought as he absorbed the warmth of the morning sun.

"Shortly we will be gazing on the perfection of all men. The power to run, jump, throw, race and compete in every way." His voice sounded slightly more like that to which Kat was accustomed.

As they walked Plouton explained that he had purchased a home nearer his own to house his hetaerae* several years ago. He would provide for his well being and all his freedom given the understanding that he would come as often as he liked, to please himself. These conditions would afford Kat solitude, an education and only one erastes*. He considered every word understanding that there was no other option.

The Demoniac

Darkness rose after a long day of gazing at naked competitors and increased passion was unleashed in Plouton. For the first time in the light of candles he forced Kat to remove his tunic. "You are all mine now!" His whisper was once again in the familiar barbarous tone. His hands explored all of his nakedness and chills ran through Kat. "You look like an Olympian. I knew I chose correctly." Kat remained silent and closed his eyes so that he could focus on freedom as he endured a different experience.

The very next morning Plouton woke Kat announcing that he now owned his own Olympian and there was no need for them to stay any longer. Together they had little to gather, which afforded them the luxury of boarding an early ship.

Once aboard, Kat was bombarded with the memories of Ponos and Thynomenos. The words and the laughter. He had no idea where they were headed but, everything felt familiar.

He forced his thoughts to Aria. Her laughter which brought with it infectious joy. Her deep green eyes like a welcome pasture and her hair a waterfall at night. She was always the most beautiful girl in the choosing room. The sun reflecting on the water and the soft motion of the ship lulled him into a place of profound peace. He daydreamed of marrying Aria on the portico of the temple of Aphrodite at sunset. The most beautiful place with the most beautiful girl. She could wear flowers in her hair and a long fiery red veil that would gently blow in the breeze. Then the two would run away together forever. A ship could take them to another world where no one would hurt them or say mean things to them.

"Seventeen steps to Aria…" Kat said aloud.

"What?" Plouton's husky voice brought him back to the brutal truth.

"Huh?" Kat hadn't realized he had spoken aloud.

"Seventeen steps to Aria? Who is Aria?" Kat stared up into his cold black eyes. "Need I remind you that you belong to me? I freed you from the temple! Now you bring pleasure only to me. No more forced ritual. Just you and me." Kat thought he glimpsed a smile above Plouton's graying beard.

He had never taken the time to study his face. It matched his voice. He was gruff looking; somewhat like a bear. He was slightly plump, and his arms bore thick hair as did his legs. His eyes were black and matched most of his hair. The gray came in streaks and defined his face.

The Demoniac

Kat wondered as he used to do, what this man was like outside of the special room. "Are you married?" He asked inquisitively.

"I have a wife, yes." He looked at Kat questioningly as he considered where the query had come from.

"And children? Do you have children?"

"Why the interrogation?"

"Well, I thought I'd like to know more about the man that chose me to be his hetaeros. Do you?"

Plouton shook his head and shifted from side to side while taking a deep breath. "Boy, you need to know nothing more than what pleases me." He took a long look at the deflated child and recognized a mark on his neck that had been missed in the darkened chambers of ritual exhortation. He couldn't take his eyes off of it. Somewhere in the back of his mind he knew it was familiar, but he just couldn't place the reason.

Kat became increasingly uncomfortable and wiped his neck. "What is it?"

"That mark."

"Mark?" Kat had not seen himself except once at the bath house as he passed. He had noticed that he was bigger than those in the lineup but, the mirror was across the room and he was requested before he could get a good look at his reflection. "I have never seen it."

"Never?"

"No… What should I call you? Do I call you Plouton or do you have a better name?"

"A better name? A better name! Plouton is a powerful name and those who are aware of me know that I am a power to be reckoned with! I am Plouton, the wealthiest man in Gerasa! Everyone knows my name and it commands respect! I do not need a better name!" He glared at Kat.

"I… I'm sorry. I didn't mean anything. I, uh, just, well, I was called Kat at the temple and I thought maybe you had also been using a different name."

"What is your given name?"

"Kataramenos."

"Zeus, Almighty! That is your name?"

"Yes," Kat timidly replied.

The Demoniac

"Why are you cursed by the gods?"

"I don't know." Kat looked at the floor and fiddled with his hands. "I used to be called Katara. Can I use that name again?"

"Cursed? I will not call you Katara. It does not bring me pleasure. I look at your soft brown hair and luscious brown skin and I see one who resembles a god not one cursed by them."

Kat was unsure of how to respond so he just looked up and smiled before turning his attention to the sea, pondering the conversation. It switched quickly from one subject to the next and he landed on something Plouton said; *"I am Plouton, the wealthiest man in Gerasa. That is where I came from. The temple of Aphrodite. The nice woman that left me there. He focused on her for several minutes. She was kind and she had other children. Why did she not want me? He studied her voice and her face as she said she was sorry, she was tired looking. Did she give me away because I'm cursed? His thoughts took him to a dark night on a mat with other children. He recalled the hushed angry voice of a man, but he couldn't recall his face.*

"He is not ours anyway, and that was the deal. He is three and we don't need more children. I will not raise another man's boy."

The Demoniac

"But I do not know who his father is."

"His mother provided the funds for three years and that time has come."

"Leave him at the marketplace someone may take him home."

"Or he will starve to death."

"Or he will starve to death, but he will not be taking food from my children."

Who is my mother? Why did she give me to them? Who is my father? How can I find out? I am cursed, no one wants me. Plouton wants me. He paid money to take me with him. Kat looked across the deck at his erastes. He did look important, and the other men did all he requested quickly. There was something about him that was frightening yet at this moment everything felt right.

Chapter 20

The home Kat lived in was small but inviting. Plouton mentioned that this was purchased years ago for hetaerae. There were no clothes and Kat had only one tunic, so money was left to purchase another as well as food. He had never been to a marketplace before, nor had he ever purchased anything. Everything had always been provided by the guides at the temples in which he served.

He became very excited to venture out on his own. He followed the sound of many voices. Turning a corner, he walked directly into the center of the marketplace. A new and oppressive sense took over. The large number of people and the sound of them bartering loudly was too much and he froze. Deep breaths and sweaty palms brought on wild thoughts of escape routes.

Food! I have to find food! Find food and leave! His eyes darted from one shop to the next. *Four shops on the left. Count the steps. I can do this. One, two, three...seventeen. Seventeen steps to food. Seventeen. Seventeen, Aria.* His breathing calmed and he found foods he knew. *Figs, goat cheese, bread, nuts, dates, olives, and pomegranates.* He knew these would taste good and sustain him. As he paid for the food, he noticed a clothing shop with tunics and cloaks hanging at the edge of the tent. As he approached the shop he froze, again. Beside the cloak, hung a scarf with the Great Bear stitched at the edge. *I must have that. My mother is a part of the Great Bear. She is looking out for me. I remember. I remember... the Great Bear!*

"I must have that. My mother is a part of the Great Bear and she is watching me. I need the scarf."

The woman running the shop glared at him coldly as he gently ran his finger over the beautiful handiwork.

"It is costly child." She snarled.

Kat said he would pay what he had left and showed her the coins in his hand. She smiled and swiftly grabbed all of them yanking the scarf down and tossing it at him. "Well, I need a tunic as well. I had enough for both."

"You said you would give me all you had left for it. You now have nothing left with which to pay for the tunic." She turned and hid the coins as she walked to the next customer. All eyes were on him and he was terrified.

Kat walked away not knowing what to do. He had meant to purchase more after purchasing the tunic and cloak. He had only enough food for a few days and now no more even to purchase more food. He wrapped the cloak around himself and slowly headed home.

Plouton did not visit for several weeks and Kat was weak from hunger when he came which infuriated him. The money he left should have been plenty to cover the cost of food and clothing yet here lay a boy losing weight and no longer resembling a god, but a street urchin.

"I will not keep you if you will not eat and train."

"I'm sorry. A lady took all my coins for a scarf."

"A scarf?" He bellowed.

Kat had already found comfort in being wrapped in it so he lifted the corner to show him what he was talking about. He knew to look up at night to find the Great Bear, but now he stared at the embroidered constellation.

"What use is that? Scarves like that are for women and besides, it is becoming cold, and you have no food and no cloak!" With that he reached his long hairy arm out and ripped the scarf from Kat's body.

"I came for you to bring me some solace in my chaos and now I have to tend to you. All because of this rag!" He raised it up and ripped it in half throwing it furiously down beside Kat's sobbing body. "Let's go!" He yanked Kat up by the arm and forced him out of the house. It took a few minutes for Kat to get his bearings. His red eyes could barely focus through the tears. The shops were closing and not many people were around which helped his anxiety.

The first shop with food was where they stopped and Plouton snatched up several items throwing coins down to pay without a word. The next stop was the garment shop in which the woman stole all the coins from Kat. Kat whispered into his ear and Plouton boisterously let everyone in the Market know what she had done and that he nor anyone employed by him would ever purchase her wares. She apologized repeatedly, bowing as he marched on to the next garment shop and proudly paid everything the merchant requested without any bartering. Now he would have a warm cloak a new chiton and plenty of food. The bug-eyed woman with the scarves scowled at Kat as they passed by once again.

Once home, Plouton watched as Kat removed the old dirty tunic and before he could replace it Plouton ravished his young body throwing him onto the

The Demoniac

floor, letting him know with certainty that this was a one-sided relationship.

Tears burned his eyes and streaked his dusty face. He cried out mentally to Aphrodite, Artemis, Zeus and any other god that would listen. "Save me from this life! Save me from this man! Let me join my mother in the Great Bear!"

Wrapped in the torn scarf he curled up on his bed and fell asleep.

Chapter 21

Days merged into months and years without anyone to talk to most of the time. He had attended classes at the gymnasium but was ignored by everyone because of his station in life. He worked tirelessly at home on his strength and compared himself silently to the athletes training for the next Olympics.

Daily, he admired his progress in the mirror someone had left at his home. He deeply loved it realizing that it was a luxury not many were afforded. He would meander through the marketplace monthly seeing other mirrors that were not nearly as intricately etched and not able to present as clear a reflection.

The Olympics were only a few short months away and he longed to join others in the competitions. He now understood the cruel words and laughter of Thynomenos all those years ago.

His particular lifestyle was not one that the average person considered worthy of upstanding citizens and therefore he was not allowed to compete, let alone own land. He was thought to be less than everyone else.

The Demoniac

Plouton was pleased with his muscular anatomy and couldn't care less about his ability to work mathematical problems quicker in his head than others did with the abacus. He cared not that Kat, now called Katara by everyone other than him was a scientific genius according to his philosophical educators. *At least...* he thought *something pleased him.*

Chapter 22

On a particularly gray day, a week before the contenders were to leave their homes, each with hopes of returning as the one crowned with laurel, knowing they had pleased Zeus, Katara pleaded again to the gods to give him favor and allow him to compete on Mount Olympus. He stared at the beloved mirror etched with the image of Zeus and bowed before it.

"I have indeed fallen into this station in life. This was not what I would have chosen for myself. My master is wealthy and gave generously to Aphrodite for my service to him. I will leave here soon, and my desire is to prove my worth to you, Great Zeus, on your glorious mountain. I implore you, oh powerful one, give me this pleasure."

He rose, picked up the bed and raised it high above his head to show off for himself and for his deity. Before returning it to its place, he saw a small box buried under where it had been. Balancing the bed on his right hand and shoulder like Atlas, he knelt and dug the box out with his left hand.

Sitting on the stool before the vanity which was the place in the room exposed to the most light, he admired the handiwork on the box. It felt familiar although, he was certain he had never seen it before. The tiny lock was easily broken as Katara determined it obviously belonged to him since he had lived here for nearly four years and no one had ever attempted to retrieve it.

Inside he found a letter written with delicate penmanship.

Sweet child,

I will give birth to you soon. The iatrine says the chances are great that I will not survive but, I want you to know about me. My favorite place to be in all the world is before my mirror. {He glanced toward the mirror wandering if it were the same one.} *I spend hours before it, brushing my long black hair and recreating the stories of Zeus and Calisto in my mind. I bore the same name, Kallisto with the K in order to honor her. I have been told frequently that I am as lovely as she must have been.*

The mirror was purchased from Joseph, a merchant from beyond the Sea of Galilee. He was born in Arimathea but settled in Capernaum. One day I hope you can travel to meet him. He is a kind man. He told me of a god named Adonai.

Adonai came to me last night. He told me that you belong to him. I am not sure what that means but, I hope it is good. As I write I am filled to overflowing with joy to know that you will have a better life than me.

I was given to Artemis when I was five, after my first dance of the bear. My parents believed that by giving me to the gods they would be blessed with health and wealth. I suppose in a way I am giving you to a god as well but, Joseph made me believe that his god is truly good.

I have two sisters and four brothers as I write this letter, but there may be more later. We are from Pella. You are probably aware of all of this since my sister, Desma, promised to take care of you and give you this letter I have written.

I imagine you as a child and wish I could raise you myself. I always believed that I would someday join the stars of the Great Bear but, Adonai said I will be with him forever in an even better place.

Katara became rigid and sat motionless. He stared at the words before walking over to the mirror and tenderly running his large hands over the etchings. *This woman lived here and looked into this mirror as I do,* he thought.

Calisto, Zeus' lover, a beautiful young nymph. This writer bore her name and dreamed of the Great Bear... The Great Bear...I wonder... when she lived here.

His eyes were drawn back to the page and he continued to read.

Since I served at the temples as a young girl, I would never have been able to marry so becoming a hetaera to the wealthy Plouton was my best and honestly my only option. He was not a kind man. He was not even a nice man, but he did provide for me. He gave me the opportunity to study at the gymnasium and bought this house for me. I hope that he changed his mind about raising you as his own. He is your father without any question. You may even look like him. I hope you have some of my features as well. I love you. Your very blessed mother, Kallisto.

I have enclosed a picture of me drawn by Petros, an artist whom I love dearly.

Katara stared at the stunning girl in the picture. Her eyes sparkled through the graphite. He imagined that the lavishly long hair felt silky from the constant brushing before the treasured mirror. She was exquisite, even in black and white. He envisioned the scene; her long delicate peplos flowing in the breeze as she strolled nonchalantly away from Petros, turning her head playfully back to smile at her true love. This life like drawing told the entire story.

"Wait!" He exclaimed aloud to an empty room. "Her neck!" He rushed to the mirror and turned his head to the right stretching to see the dark spot he had from birth. He reached his left hand up and rubbed it and looked back at the drawing. He was certain it was the same as the picture. He studied the mirror and the picture for several long minutes.

"Kallisto," he whispered, "are you my mother?" His thoughts raced wildly. Who could tell him for sure? *She must have left a clue in the letter*, he thought. He reread every word. *Joseph, a merchant from Capernaum is quite far. Petros, a common name and no telling where he would be found. She was at the temple of Artemis, maybe someone there would know something.*

Chapter 23

The darkness had come quickly last night, and he was unable to sleep because today could reveal much. He ran all the way to the temple. He showed the picture to a few women and finally stood before Aphrodesia. She smiled the moment she saw him.

"Kataramenos," her voice was melodic and her form stunning. Her smile calmed his racing heart.

"You know me?"

"Yes, you look just like your mother. I had hoped that you would find me one day."

"My mother?" His heart beat so hard it felt like it was going to burst from his chest cavity.

"Kallisto,"

Her voice, the name, like a melodious song.

Kallisto was my mother? Delight and confusion melded in his thoughts. Kallisto… and Plouton… that cannot be! "Is there another Plouton in Gerasa?" He blurted out. He hoped the answer would put his anguished thoughts to rest.

"No, Kataramenos, there is not one." She tilted her head and squinted ever so slightly as she tried to read his mind. "I'm sorry, Kataramenos. It seems you have already met Plouton."

"Yes" he snarled. The burning fury returned and to such great height there was no boundary found in him. He left without another word. He had never been to Plouton's home, but he knew he could not wait for him to visit.

With every step, rage grew fiercer within him. "Plouton" he spoke in a gruff growling voice unlike his own. The man in front of him fearfully pointed past the marketplace. Kataramenos stormed through the crowded streets muttering about his mother's kindness, beauty and undeserved lot in life. He found himself outside the town and his wrath was almost tangible as he approached another man. "Plouton!" he roared at the stranger; terror filled his eyes and he timidly pointed further down the road.

"Kataramenos!" he began, "son of Kallisto, the beautiful nymph, lover of Zeus and hetaera of Plouton." His voice was becoming deep and more guttural as he continued the conversation with himself. Throwing his fists in the air he screamed. "Kataramenos, son of the wealthy Plouton, hetaeros of the wicked Plouton!" He let out a fierce howl and fell to the ground. He wanted to cry; however, his head twisted left then right several times and he let out a thunderous roar followed by an unnaturally high jump to his feet. Bolting forward with the speed of a leopard, he approached a swineherd* who stumbled backward as swiftly as possible without taking his eyes off the man/creature in front of him.

"Plouton!" He hissed and stretched out to bat the young man to the ground. The stench of pig dung escaped his senses as he focused on the scrawny finger of the terrified adolescent pointing further down the road. As he looked in that direction, he saw another figure running toward a house in the distance.

Plouton was to the gate before Kataramenos arrived. He appeared filthy and puny to him now. "What do you think you are doing here?" Plouton's voice filled with a quiet superiority. "You are never to come near my home."

Kataramenos reached out and scratched his arm, shredding his cloak and drawing blood. Every bitterness arose to the surface as he roared again like a lion. "Kallisto was my mother!"

With that Plouton deeply understood the entirety of his young eromenos' actions. Instantly he was face to face with his own unforgivable actions. All along he felt like the mark on his neck was familiar but had never attempted to understand why.

"Kat," trying to calm him, he put up both hands and motioned downwardly as if to silently settle the situation.

"Kataramenos!" He thundered in return. Several of the servants surrounded him and he remained singularly focused.

"I'm sorry about your mother. It was not my fault that she died." He distracted him as four men jumped on top of the stranger attacking their master. He lay on the ground unaware of the pain of their repeated blows. Plouton looked down and continued, with disgust, "It was your fault!" He spat in his face and motioned to his servants before turning to walk back to his home.

The servants lifted him to his feet, dragged him away from the house so that it would not frighten the family and beat him severely. Left alone at the far corner of the pig fields where they dragged his body, he slept.

Awakened by pigs sniffing him and nibbling at his feet he dragged himself to the nearest tree. Using all his available strength he pulled himself up and vowed to the pigs to take revenge.

Chapter 24

Kataramenos surrendered more each day to new animalistic behaviors. Plouton no longer visited, therefore he no longer supported him. No money for food sent him out at night in search of scraps thrown out by merchants or families at the end of long days.

Confronted by wild dogs he would fight for and win bits of meat or fish behind homes. In fact, his only delight was the frequency and quantity of food wasted by families in town.

Time passed quickly during the cooling of summer and travelers returned home with stories of the illustrious Olympians. He crouched behind bushes and soaked up the last warmth of sun each day as he listened to all the news.

He imagined himself to be the swiftest and most agile competitor. He could almost feel the laurel wreath crowning his head. He would fantasize about the exaggerated roar of the crowd as he strolled to the center of the arena.

The nights were getting colder as summer ended and winter approached. He continued to occupy the home in which his mother had given him life, until

The Demoniac

Plouton returned from the Olympic games with a new hetaeros. Kataramenos had not spoken to anyone in several weeks. He displayed accelerated strength and aggression toward Plouton and his new boy. So much so that they both retreated. The boy stayed at a nearby inn for the night with a promise from Plouton to evict Kataramenos promptly.

Kataramenos had no fear, but he preempted the impending fight with the removal of his possessions. He carefully hid the mirror and the treasure box containing his mother's letter and picture to a secluded spot outside of town.

Returning to retrieve the clothes and bed he was met by five servants. He tried to run but the men caught up to him they beat him and left him to die, throwing stones as they left.

Shame and fear at his retreat gripped him so severely that he ripped leaves and bark from a nearby bush branch and beat himself; shrieking, howling and hissing with each lash. The pain on the already bruised muscles was unbearable, but he knew he deserved every lash. Exhausted and bloody he fell to the dirt beneath him.

There was no way for him to know how long he had lain in that place. Blood and dirt dried together, and his legs refused to hold him upright. He slowly dragged his weakened body to a nearby tree and leaned up against it. In his mind, he retraced the blurry memory of the hours before passing out. Uncertain of how he had gotten to this particular location and why he had been so brutally beaten, he focused on the time at the temple when Malleus informed him that he had lost ten days for a second time. Those were frightening and painful memories, fractured as they were.

How many days had he lost this time? With no one close to him there would never be a way of knowing. Tears burned his lacerated cheeks. His lips cracked as dehydration usurped his body causing disorientation.

Water, I need water, or I will die. Where am I? He looked around, attempting to figure out where he was. *Water,* he repeated in his head, *I must find water.*

Struggling to his feet, he made his way along a narrow briar-lined path searching for life sustaining water. He studied the sky for a brief moment as a chill filled the air.

It is mid-morning, he thought, taking in the sun's location. Every step compounded the pain, so he concentrated solely on the search for water. After what felt like hours, he heard water trickling over stones and old leaves. Desperate for a cool taste of water his pace quickened.

Initially, the cold water was a shock to his senses; nevertheless he lapped water while intermittently dunking, his face fully into the stream.

Raising slightly, the recognizable grunting of pigs caught his attention, thus jolting fragments of memory to the forefront of his mind. Men beating him, Plouton's face in his, and a stranger beside them. Leaves and bark and animals crying in pain, unthinkable pain.

What animals howled, screeched and even hissed, he wondered. His stomach rumbled, making him acutely aware of his hunger.

I do not think I am near a town. Where will I find food? His thoughts were interrupted by the sight of a minnow in the brook and with lightening reflex it was caught and in his mouth. *Barely a bite,* he thought. *I require more than that.* The grunting got louder so he crawled into a bush close by, escaping the view of the pigs and their keeper. A gasp escaped his mouth as he caught sight of the familiar servant.

I am on Plouton's land, the thought was so loud in his head he feared being discovered. Several pigs passed him, and he didn't care to count them. Food was his only thought. *I will wait till nightfall then I will capture and eat one,* he promised himself. *Taking what should be rightfully mine is not wrong,* he reasoned.

He rested, well hidden in the brush until the moon rose over the horizon and the sun was asleep.

Silently he crept to a sleeping sow and with no remorse smashed her head with a very large stone.

At morning's light, the servants followed a bloody trail to the edge of the brook and then it disappeared from their sight. Each of the swineherds swore an oath to keep this loss a secret. Plouton was a fierce master and there was no need to cause his wrath to befall them over a single sow. He has hundreds, they agreed.

Kataramenos had dragged the carcass far away and built a fire eating to his heart's content. The meat was plenty for several days before it became rancid. He shared his food with several curious animals that bravely approached.

Over the next several weeks he perfected the kill. The colder weather brought longevity to the meat. Tiring of pork, he ate wild animals that had once shared his meals.

The Demoniac

The winter tarried and he had taken clothing from lines on which they were drying, to keep from freezing. If anyone saw him, he would flail his arms and howl prior to chasing them, thus inciting fear to towns reaching from Gerasa to Gedara. Men were enlisted to hunt him down and kill him. A few brave men volunteered while others dismissed the stories as myths.

Chapter 25

Kataramenos roamed the countryside drifting from small town to small town. His thoughts grew wilder and angrier as time passed. He had been captured a few times over the years. Once, men bound him with cords and tied his arms and legs to a tree expecting a lion to ravage him. Before they had gotten too far away, they heard the roar of a lion and turned to watch. However, the roar was that of their prey as he broke the cords and chased them. He finally tired of their screams and pleas for mercy, and he smugly turned and disappeared.

The story had incited a surge of men attempting to prove their fearless valor. Chains were the choice for groups of men confident in their ability to subdue Kataramenos. Once a group of six men approached the demoniac, as he had been labeled, their laughter and chain rattles, drew him from his place of solitude. *A new game, I will show them what I am capable of,* he thought. He rushed toward the group, which was beyond their expectations. He roared like the king of beasts; then jumped as high as the tallest of them. Three of them held out the chains arranging them like a net to capture the beast/man.

The Demoniac

The relentless tormenting, poking and laughter halted abruptly as he rose and broke the chains. He became the trapper and they the hunted. His eyesight narrowed in on the slowest of the pack, pouncing like a jackal. The slowest now bound in chain, wept and begged for help. Kataramenos laughed a fiendish laugh which solidified his entire being.

That laugh! He realized, *is the laugh of the cruel ones of my youth. It is the laugh of the spirits in the darkness. I just did that!* He was horrified.

Chapter 26

Walking for hours, darkness surrounded him like a thick blanket, and he finally dropped from pure exhaustion. The moon was absent from the sky as he searched for the Great Bear.

"Mama!" He cried aloud to the vast night sky. His first words in years. "Mama, I am scared!" He covered his face and sobbed, terrified of who or what he had become.

Another fitful night of horror as he slept. There had not been rest ever since he could remember, and the nightmares had intensified since he had been enlightened as to who his father was.

Light peaked in, ever so delicately reaching his face through vines and leaves hanging down in front of him. Where had he traveled this time? he wondered. Realizing the temporary home he slept in was a small cave, he inched his way out cautiously on all fours. The sun's scorching rays burned his eyes as he emerged from the darkness. Momentarily blinded, he kept his eyes closed as he stretched. Rubbing sleep from his eyes he searched the landscape for clues as to his whereabouts. Nothing looked familiar, which spoke volumes since wandering the Decapolis had taken him nearly everywhere for longer than he could clearly comprehend.

He heard the scurry of a small rodent at his feet and before he had time to think about his actions he snatched it up and bit into it.

The familiar sound of hunters after several days of silence reminded him of his fate. Living among the tombs and punishing only himself led him to imagine the world had given up on capturing the "demoniac."

"Yes, I am sure! Word spread that the neighbor of a friend of my uncle's sister's husband saw him a few nights ago, creeping around on all fours like the animal he is," came a tenor voice.

"But here? These are tombs. I don't even want to go over there in the daytime," came a deeper voice.

"What if we see a ghost?" Man number three, Kataramenos noted.

"Hush! Where would you expect the cursed one to live?" The first man's voice silenced the others.

Kataramenos howled and ran to an easy spot to surprise his prey. He laughed the fiendish laugh and screamed in a high-pitched female tone. The footsteps stopped directly in front of his trap. He snorted like an angry bull and watched as they all instantly faced his hole; then he plunged out of the dark cave toward them. He swung the jaw of a former meal at them and laughed the most terrifying laugh anyone had ever heard, including him.

An arrow struck his left shoulder, and a dagger caught his right forearm. The vigilantes had no idea the tremendous pain he endured daily as he sliced his skin to shreds watching blood stream out, hoping that each day would be his last.

A crowd that had followed the vigilantes at a distance stood frozen in fear as the cursed; part animal, part man pulled the arrow from his shoulder and sliced open a place next to the one made with the dagger. He breathed deeply and then let out a blood-curdling scream.

Every man scattered in a different direction. He chased two men and leapt toward them catching a foot of each of them bringing the pair down with a loud thud, taking their breath from them. He then threw them toward the secret meet-up spot they told discussed before they knew he was listening.

"He is dead!" One man yelled to the others before the next victim fell from the sky.

The Demoniac

"He killed them both!" The leader bellowed. "Run for your lives!"

"Kataramenos!" thundered the demoniac, "Kataramenos!"

Chapter 27

The following day a young man crept out cautiously from a cave close to the boisterous Kataramenos. He had chosen to live there a few weeks before this hideous creature arrived. Previously he had been orphaned, left to his own devices on the streets of Gedara. He had been spit on, cursed, beaten and raped. There had not ever in his recollection been anyone that cared if he lived or died. He regularly stole food from merchants in order to survive. This burial ground was near water and the caves were off-limits to "normal" society.

He scurried like a small animal along the base of the trees from one hole to the next, all the time keeping an eye on who or whatever this Kataramenos was. Laying a handful of olives and 2 figs in front of him as an offering of peace then slinking back into his cave, Cassius watched to see if his offering would be accepted.

Kataramenos watched the small figure scurry like a frightened animal, then grunted as he tasted the delicious fruits laid before him. His mind grasped at reasons for such an act of kindness. Not coming up with any reasons he knelt down and put his face into the cave he had seen the boy enter. "Why?" he asked in a normal tone.

The boy, who could not speak, shrugged and began to make signals toward him and grunted and growled before hiding his face.

Kataramenos laughed a frighteningly unnatural laugh and moved away from the cave with a motion for the young man to exit and join him.

Cassius stayed fully hidden until night then discretely went to hunt for food. Kataramenos lay in a rut with his head on a tree root silently watching his newly discovered companion.

The morning sun woke both of them and together they ate all Cassius had scrounged from the ground near the marketplace down the road. Bits of fish, figs, pomegranates, bread, grapes and olives, enough to fill them.

Together they chased the swineherds from Plouton's farm. Occasionally, one of them would be caught and Kataramenos would break chains to free whichever one was caught, then they would chase off the guards, allowing them to enjoy roasted pig for days.

The Demoniac

The fearsome and fearful, an unlikely relationship, but each found the companionship for which they longed.

Days turned to months and the summer was again giving way to the winter. Kataramenos took Cassius to Plouton's home and using his covert skills, Cassius pilfered warm cloaks for each of them, while Kataramenos secured a goat and a couple of chickens. Undiscovered, they made their way back to the tombs. Winter would be difficult but, both of them had survived worse.

The towns became more densely populated and the stories of the defiant beast living in the cliff of tombs by the sea were heard by everyone.

Rarely a brave sailor would wander near and "barely escape with his soul yet in his body," as was becoming the saying of the time. They were living nightmares for communities far beyond their inclination to roam.

The Demoniac

Part two

The Demoniac

The Demoniac

Chapter 28

The day had been like any other of late. Long hours and crowds surrounded Jesus and His followers. He taught in parables all day even though they were often not easily understood everyone listened intently. Wide eyed and silent curious families sat as words were absorbed. Young children played quietly as older ones sat reverently listening to the charismatic rabbi. The numbers in the gatherings had increased exponentially from the beginning of His ministry. His full-time followers had also grown in number from a handful to over 70 so it took quite a bit more effort to enter a city covertly. On days like this one they were met by large crowds in the outskirts of town and while Jesus tirelessly spoke with genuine concern and deep wisdom, ten to fifteen of His closest friends would enter the nearest town and purchase necessities for the continuing journey while the others were in charge of crowd control. One never knew how long the crowds would remain, sometimes the majority would linger for several days while stragglers stopped to listen for a few hours then move on. Many times, Jesus would only have the opportunity to eat late in the evening or early morning. Often, he would fast for 2 to 3 days at a time. The women that had devoted themselves to the care of Him and His core group would frequently prepare meals for them. None of them ever had to purchase sandals or clothing because just when new attire was necessary someone would approach with a tale of being awakened by a dream of the need. Visits with Jesus' dear friend, Lazarus and his two sisters, Mary and Martha, culminated in farewell gifts of food and finances.

A fisherman that had seen the miracle that happened for Peter and his brother Andrew donated the use of one of his ships to Jesus to be at His ready whenever He needed one. That morning He told Peter, Andrew, James and John to prepare it for a trip across the Sea of Galilee. As they worked together, they expressed an odd feeling that something strange was about to happen. They had grown accustomed to previously unimaginable new miracles and fresh unexplored teachings, but today they all felt a tangible tension. The crowd was growing restless and more left sooner than usual.

"Jesus!" Mary cried out pleadingly, "I have to reach him," she repeated as she pushed through the crowd. Word was sent to Jesus' disciple Bartholomew that Jesus' mother had arrived and was desperately trying to get to him. Jesus smiled and said aloud that His mother and brothers were all those that listened and put his lessons to use, placing everyone on a comfortable common ground.

The Demoniac

"Jesus!" Mary called out all the louder. The crowd opened slowly as many realized who she was, and whispers accompanied each shout.

Bartholomew escorted Mary to the edge of the crowd, allowing for a private meeting with her son. Thomas, Judas, James the Lesser, and Matthew ushered the crowd away from the shore while Phillip, Nathaniel and James prepared food for the journey ahead. Jesus excused Himself and went to His mother.

The women that would normally be with them were asked to go home for a few days. This provided time to give families and friends some insights and updates. Those around Capernaum that desired to do so also gave regular offerings to support the Rabbi of Love. He had earned this new title by the sermons and parables he preached all over. He had gone to the Samaritans and many there had decided to follow His teachings as well. This was unheard of since they were obviously impure half-breeds. None of them had been allowed to worship at the temple since the exile when many had married Gentiles. The Samaritans were now only partly Jewish and any respectable Jew would stay clear of them. Jesus, however, walked right in as though they were equal to everyone else. He spoke of love and grace to those who had never experienced it. His acceptance of those poor undesirables along with the many times

The Demoniac

He healed the untouchable lepers and basically anybody, gave Him the right to be called the Rabbi of Love.

The 70 surrounding the Rabbi regularly had been commissioned to leave everything and follow in order to gain wisdom as they went, but today Jesus asked that He be left with only the inner circle of twelve.

A ship was docked down the shore and prepared for at least 20 to follow from a distance.

"Jesus," Mary said frantically when they finally met, "I had a dream,"

"It is ok Eema*," Jesus spoke in an unequaled calming voice.

"No! No, my son. It was real!"

"I know, Eema."

"No, Jesus, I mean it!" She demanded, "A ferocious animal like man wants to kill you."

Jesus smiled and nodded, touching her shoulder he repeated "Yes, Eema, I know, but My Father has already prepared the way. There is no need to worry,

Eema. Nothing can happen without my Father's allowance."

"Jesus, I…" She bent her head and sighed as she wondered if continuing was the right thing to do. Looking into His eyes she was immediately at ease.

"You are a great Eema." Jesus reassured her with a hug before turning to board the ship.

It was not a large ship, but plenty big enough for 20 to 30 passengers and a crew. Jesus told His disciples that they were to cross Galilee in order to meet someone. He went to the stern and lay on a cushion to rest. The men were not sure if it was to rest from the day or for the next event.

They looked across the water and saw that the small boat and 3 small fishing vessels had launched. They grumbled among themselves about the lack of obedience and respect from some of the other followers.

"Who do you think we will meet?" Thomas asked anyone who would listen. Everyone shrugged their shoulders and looked at each other.

"There is no telling with Him, you know?" James started and then was distracted by lightning.

The Demoniac

Matthew gasped and was instantly unable to catch his breath at the sight of excessive lightning in the direction they were headed. The others all screamed, waved and pointed at the smaller vessels closer to shore, attempting to warn them of the impending danger. Within 5 minutes a powerful wind dropped down causing their ship to tip from side to side forcing the mast to intersect with one of the surrounding walls of water.

Fear aggressively seized the hearts of all 12 men, even those who had made a living on the sea. All of them began to shout for Jesus. The sound of the storm inhibited the sound of voices. The water pounded the boat destructively. Peter let go of the side of the ship and ran to the stern to wake Jesus. At this moment he didn't feel the bravest, but he was the closest. In that moment the water changed with the wind to a swirling motion. Terrified screams came from the helpless men. Peter leaned in close to Jesus' ear and yelled above the storm, "Jesus! How can you sleep? Don't you care at all that we are all about to die?"

Jesus woke and looked around, "Are you serious? Where is your faith? Have you been with me all this time and still unable to trust in The Word?" His voice penetrated the chaos and exposed each heart. "Peace!" he said in a natural tone. He raised His hands and continued, "Be still!"

The Demoniac

In the blink of an eye the water was calm, and the tempest stilled. Every man stared at the man in front of them in awe. Wonder filled their thoughts as they considered silently who He actually was and what they had witnessed.

The other boats were safe and back on the shore and all passengers were disembarking. The ship on which the disciples rode had somehow not changed course in all the disruption. Miracle after miracle and every one of them an unprecedented phenomenon.

How is it that we are not all dead? Judas Iscariot wondered.

That was impossible! The air and the sea? Thomas shook his head as he thought.

Every thought mirrored the others' and no one spoke.

Jesus, knowing their thoughts, said "That you may know the Word is Truth. The power of life and death are in the tongue."

No one said a word the rest of the trip.

Chapter 29

As the boat neared the shore, they smelled the distinct odor of rotting flesh. Jesus was praying so they did not disturb Him, instead they prepared to dock.

Blood chilling screams and deep mournful groans sent shivers down their spines and ice into their veins. The fear they had experienced in the storm returned, however, Jesus got out and began to walk toward the nearby cliff of tombs where the noise was centered. With silent reluctance everyone followed.

"Aaaaaahhhh!" A man jumped out from behind a tree screaming in a deep growl. The groans came from a distance behind him. Everyone looked for a second man, but only Matthew caught a glimpse of the naked man peeking out from a cave.

Kataramenos' eyes fell on Jesus and he dropped to his knees bowing his face to the ground, forcibly worshiping.

Jesus commanded "Come out of the man!"

"Have you come to torture us? It is not yet time."

The Demoniac

"What is your name?" Jesus asked, undisturbed by the foul smelling, naked, growling individuals.

"Legion!" They roared in one, yet multiple voices, emanating from the one before them. "We are many!"

The man twisted and pointed to a large herd of pigs. "Jesus, Son of the Most High, if we must leave these bodies, allow us to use the bodies of those."

Jesus nodded and everyone watched as what appeared to be billows of both opaque and translucent clouds rushed toward the pigs, a hundred feet away.

The pigs squealed in pain and horror running swiftly toward the cliff and jumping willingly into the sea, splattering on the rocks or drowning.

Twelve sets of eyes stared at Kataramenos without moving or speaking, they tried to wrap their minds around this inexplicable situation.

Matthew was the first to move, offering a tunic to the smaller man, now sitting on a large stone.

Andrew silently approached the louder, larger man offering him a tunic. Kataramenos and Cassius dressed and fell at the feet of Jesus worshiping through tears. His tender smile let his disciples know that all was well. They couldn't fathom how but knew that everything was finished.

"Go and get food while we talk." He said to the twelve. Obediently, they left. Along the way they discussed the recent events and the uniqueness of them. They were so pleased and excited that they were chosen to be a part of all that had happened and what was still to come.

Chapter 30

"Kataramenos," Jesus spoke with more compassion than he had ever heard. "Cassius," He continued, "I am He who takes away the sins of the world. I have come today to set you both free." The two men cried uncontrollably as they bowed at his feet, this time in their right minds and fully willing.

"You are no longer the cursed of the gods, you will no longer be called Kataramenos, but Theodore, for you were a gift to my Father in Heaven by your mother before you were born, and today you are blessed by Him with righteousness." He turned to Cassius as Theodore wept with joy.

"Cassius, you will no longer be hollow, but full and whole. You will be called Gaios for you are complete and made full when you rejoice."

Theodore spoke between sobs, "You are so powerful and full of mercy. I never knew of such a god. Why have you chosen me to be kind to?"

Jesus smiled and lifted each of their faces toward His. "Rise up, I have so much to say to you before we are disturbed." The men rose and sat in front of their savior on a large boulder.

"Gaios, your tongue is loose and you will forever more be able to rejoice," He began.

"Praise be unto you, my God!" Gaios exploded with the first words he had ever spoken. The sound of his husky voice surprised both men.

"Theodore, your mother was a kind woman and in the quiet of her room, she often called to the One of whom Joseph spoke. She asked Adonai for favor on her life and the life of her child.

"When I was 12, I created a cradle for a special child and gave it to Joseph in order for you to be wrapped and marked for my Father who told me exactly how it should be made."

Theodore immediately saw in his memory the tiny bed he had to leave behind when he went to the temple. He recalled the sorrow he had felt that he would no longer be safe in his bed. His eyes were opened to the loss once again until he focused on the One that had made that place of comfort. The One that had released him now from that inner feeling of discomfort, fear and insecurity. Those eyes full of the safest emotion, he could not contain or express such feelings, and tears flowed as Jesus continued.

"Both of you were cursed from birth by those who should have been giving tender care. They used their authority over you to speak death and lies into your tender souls.

"My Father heard every word, and saw every dark place you sunk into. Those places deep inside, in which you believed you could hide and be safe. He saw you, Theodore, snuggle deep into the center of your bed under the covers as you held your ears and eyes closed. Even though He allowed those most heinous actions against you to continue for these years, understand this, His angels were also there blocking the even more physically, mentally, and spiritually deadly actions the enemy had intended.

"Your eyes were opened at an early age by the demonic entities worshiped by your people, to the spirit realm so you could see and hear demons moving around in your room. This created open crevices into your spirit that those spirit creatures could enter. It was not the will of My Father for those to enter or torment you day and night.

"You are symbolic of the world now and in the future. Symbols of the depths of evil that have been and that will be. You will open the eyes of many to the extremes of depravity. The people's sense of security, joy and laughter will be removed.

"The enemy attacks the mind and the body. Fear and hatred grow in that place of darkness like unwanted vines. Today, my Father sent me to you. Today is the day of salvation. The day to release you from the dungeon of dark abomination. For the first time you are free to speak your own words, free to love and accept His love.

"Theodore, numbers have always been important to you for a reason. Numerically, 10 is a symbol of the power and authority of Adonai, My Father. When you lost 10 days three times," Theodore looked inquisitive. He wondered if this man who seemed to know everything could be mistaken regarding that number of times. Jesus smiled knowingly, "Yes, Theodore, 3 times, when you were beaten and left for dead by the servants of Plouton you again lost 10 days." Theodore's eyes widened as he remembered that event and his fleeting thought at that time. "Each time you were hidden in the Secret Place of The Most High God. His angels nursed you back to health and kept you from death that the enemy requested.

"Seventeen, not only the number of steps to Aria and to the first market for food, but also it has been 17 years since you were given to a goddess of your people." Again, Theodore smiled in disbelief. No one knew his age or his day of birth. No one had ever asked. Yet this man knew everything about him. "Yes, I know, my Father has kept me updated. It is time, He told me today. The same day as your birth is the day of your rebirth. Seventeen represents victory."

Theodore fell to his feet and kissed them repeatedly. His lifelong desire had been to be the victor at the Olympics, but this was a far greater victory! He was overcome with thankfulness. Gaios listened and watched and cried. He felt every bit of the joy his companion was feeling.

"Gaios, you were sent by the Father to be his companion. He is grateful for your willingness. You are free. Fear has no more place in you. You will live long on the earth. Your obedience rewarded as you move forward. Adonai has always had a plan and a purpose for you." He held his head in his hands as he cried uncontrollably.

"I have been seen?"

"Yes, and loved. You were given a special assignment from birth to assist Theodore. Now you are welcome to follow your dreams. You have desired to marry and create with wood as I have done. You will provide for yourself and others through your talent. Tell everyone all about what Adonai has done for you." He rose and hugged Jesus.

"Each of these chain links," He reached down beside him pulling up one of several pieces of chain littering the rocky hillside, "are here to represent your true freedom. Iron melted down and formed by fire to imprison you. They display victorious release from abyssal captivity. These will be a reminder to everyone for eons to come of the glorious fullness of the power of Adonai, the Creator of the universe."

They looked around in wonder at the hundreds of individual links scattered across the terrain, seeing heavy chains, shackles, and ropes.

Jesus knew their thoughts and continued. "These were physical representations of what was going on spiritually. Your minds trapped in disdain and rage. Your souls hidden from every source of light. Each time you would break one of these there was another to replace it." This drew their eyes back to Him as they silently questioned the longevity of their freedom.

Today, My Father released me to come to you. As we sailed into the sea the prince of the power of the air tried to overtake our ship. He feared the loss of position he has here. He used you mercilessly to wreak havoc in this region. He knew that if I made it to you his reign would be defeated. But, God, my, Father was moved with compassion for you both and for this region. His love is more powerful than the hatred, fear, and indifference ruling the Decapolis. Every moment of your lives spent in captivity by the evil one has been reclaimed. You will never again be subject to his authority. I give you the full authority of Heaven to offer freedom to everyone you come into contact with. I release to you the authority to cast out demons and heal the sick.

"My time on earth is drawing to an end. I will be betrayed and handed over to be crucified." They both interrupted with a solemn oath to protect Him with their lives. Jesus smiled tenderly and began again.

"No, my sons," their heads tilted at such an address. Neither of them had been privileged to have a father and the kindness of this man was already more than they deserved, but father?

"Yes, you are called to be sons of The Most High God. He has chosen you as His beloved." Tears formed again as they were enveloped in a love they had never known. "After 3 days and nights in the belly of the earth, I will rise from the grave. When I do, I will come to you. I say all this clearly so that you will not be confused, but sure of your faith."

"My sons, listen, they are coming. There is a back-breaking fear that erupted when those demons sent the swine to their death. There is an uncontrolled hatred eating at the hearts of the people here."

"Yes, we know."

"The Spirit of God will fill you both to go. Go into the entirety of the region to spread the news of a God that loves unconditionally and responds to a repentant heart. The One who has power and authority to release prisoners from their captors and clear the hearts and minds from every form of evil. The God of Heaven is the only one that loves enough to give His only Son to be the living sacrifice for all of humanity. You will be living testimonies to all who have known you or heard the stories. Others will be sent later to this region to testify to the truth you have spread about Adonai.

"Theodore, you are to tell everyone. Many will have their hearts changed because of your testimony. Many will be afraid of the new way of thinking. Do not be moved by their fear or their hatred, move on. You will be tilling dry and rocky soil and planting seeds of faith. Some will hear and allow their faith to grow. Some will resist and some will start to make changes allowing for new growth and then dry up being swept back into their old way of life. These results are not your concern but the concern of My Father. You go and speak and tell of the praises of God-Adonai then move on and let Him water those seeds so that others will come in and see great harvest."

Gaios rose and hugged Jesus not ever wanting to let go. The 12 were within sight and he realized his time had come so he left to explore his newfound freedom and ability to speak. "Thank you! Thank you! I will forever be your son. I will bring you pleasure. Thank you, I love you!" He shouted as he ran.

Theodore remained, overcome with gratitude and an overwhelming desire to know more. "Teach me. I am unlearned in such matters. I am unworthy of this assignment. I don't understand this love. I don't know how to wield this authority I want to know more about Adonai."

"I have done what was required of me. I have set you free. You are now open to the fullness of the love of Adonai. It is too much to learn in a few hours. He will give you 3 days in the secret place now aware of all that is happening. You will be taught by the angels. Then you will go to Joseph of Arimathea, the merchant from whom your mother learned. You will stay with him for another 3 days and he will teach you but even more importantly, you will teach him about me. I am The Messiah, the One he has waited for his entire life and you are the chosen messenger to him.

The Demoniac

The disciples arrived conversing and laughing among themselves carrying food and wine filled canteens. They quieted the closer they came, in order for Jesus to do what He did best... teach and love. "Theodore search for Joseph of Aramathea in the marketplace. Tell him all that I have told you and all I have done."

The disciples offered them food and drink then they all spoke openly of their calling. Jesus sat silently listening to the lively conversation and watching as Theodore absorbed every word. He had hungered his entire life for such friendship and sense of worth.

Chapter 31

Terror struck the countryside as news spread rapidly of a new and powerful entity. The men told of the demoniac being set free and the eerie sound of the visible wind rushing past them and into the swine they were tending. Many men joined to demand that this man leave immediately. It had taken several hours for the mob to form with enough courage to face this fierce adversary.

Shouting came from behind Jesus, Theodore and the twelve. "Hey! You! The one that sent my pigs to…" Plouton arrived followed by a throng of men, many of whom had been victims of the rage of Kataramenos. They stopped abruptly staring at the completely wicked man sitting on a stone laughing and eating, fully clothed with his hair and body perfectly clean and acting as sane as they were.

"How is this possible? Is that truly the same man? Who has that much power? How can anyone take authority against all that filled him? That kind of power is terrible and more than I want to face." The crowd whispered to each other.

Jesus nodded at Plouton, and he instantly realized that the power and authority in front of him could say the word and he would be dead. Intense fear strangled his pompous voice as he fell to his knees and bowed his face to the ground. Many, but not all followed his lead.

"Sir, I implore you to leave this region. Those were my pigs and that was the entirety of my worth. You have broken me, and I beg you to leave before more evil befalls us." He groveled without lifting his face. The others dropped to their knees. Seeing the great Plouton's respect made them understand the gravity of the situation. They too could be wiped out if this man chose to come against them. He must be a god and to have yet another god and one with such power was exponentially terrifying.

They did not repent. They did not take responsibility for their past. They thought only of their wealth and position among men.

Jesus turned to Theodore and simply said, "Move on when there is no repentance."

Behind Plouton and his men more men from Gedara approached with stones and curses. They demanded the departure of an even greater evil than that which already ruled the Decapolis.

Theodore looked out over the mob and turned again to Jesus, who was almost to the shore. "Jesus!

Please!" He plead urgently, "Please let me come with you!"

"No, Theodore, go and spread the news. I will return. And Theodore, find Aria, she has kept your memory in her heart. You are not alone, my son."

Theodore stopped dead in his tracks, Aria... he had not thought of her in years. Maybe someday they could be married and sail on a big ship far away. His thoughts were clear and his wonder for the depths and the widths and the heights and the lengths of the love of Adonai was unfathomable. He had provided for him a companion and a powerful sonship. It was mind boggling. Time stood still as Jesus and his disciples boarded their ship and set sail while curses were yelled from the cliffs. He was frozen in a bubble as if he were invisible. He saw Jesus from the ship looking at him with glorious compassion. All tension in every muscle was released and he closed his eyes, falling into liquid love and floating there while he rested his heart, mind and body.

He heard the voice of Jesus explaining that everything that happened from the beginning of time, pointed the world to Himself, the Redeemer, the promised Messiah. He envisioned Jesus' words coming to fruition; His crucifixion and His resurrection. He saw the emergence of followers of the Way filling homes in the Decapolis and faith growing in the lives of many.

Night fell and the mobs couldn't find the cursed one. They never saw him enter the boat; nonetheless they couldn't find him on shore or in the caves. As darkness moved in they broke up into small groups returning to their original starting places.

Chapter 32

Theodore was overcome with gratitude daily. Every sunrise brought a deeper understanding that he walked in a new reality. He purposed to find Aria as well as Aspasia and Aphrodesia. The time spent resting in the secret place filled with love and made him realize that Plouton had already made his choice. He came face to face with the One that could give him a true value and pleaded with him to leave.

He headed to the marketplace to find Joseph to learn all that he could about Adonai, and to in turn teach him about the Messiah.

Approaching the oddly familiar streets filled with markets he focused solely on the inner voice that sounded like Jesus. Joseph's face was familiar and his joyous voice as well.

"Joseph!" Theodore announced his arrival as if they were old friends.

"Do I know you, my friend?"

"Well, we met once when I was a child. Recently, I was told to find you by the Messiah of your people."

Joseph's eyes widened and his countenance changed.

"I have words to speak with you. A message to pass along. You are the first stop in my travels. I am here to learn from you about Adonai and to teach you about Jesus of Nazareth."

Joseph urged him to join him in his tent behind the marketplace. "You look very familiar, my friend, but you have the advantage here." He sat on a large cushion and motioned for Theodore to do the same across from him. He then offered food and wine.

"You knew my mother, Kallisto."

"Yes, yes! She was a beautiful soul." He nodded, "God rest her soul."

"You sold her a mirror and told her of a different god." Joseph nodded. "That changed her life. Jesus told me that she sat before that mirror calling out to Adonai the god that created the heavens and the earth."

Joseph laughed loudly and clapped his hands. "Praise be to Adonai."

Theodore chuckled to himself, watching the grandiosity of Joseph's animation. "She did not know much about Him. However, the night before my birth His angel visited her, and she committed her soul and mine to Him."

Joseph bowed face to floor and shouted again, "Praise be to the Great Adonai!"

"My birth caused her death and those entrusted with my care called me Kataramenos, meaning cursed of the gods. I lived my entire life living up to those words. I had been filled with a legion of demons. Men chased and chained me attempting to kill me."

Joseph clicked his tongue and shook his head in despair. "I had heard of such a man. And here you sit before me. How exactly did this happen?"

"Three days ago, a man followed by 12 others disembarked a ship at the shore of Galilee along the cliff of tombs where I lived. I had no control of my mind or body, but those inside me forced me to my knees and began to worship this man, calling him the Son of The Most High God."

Joseph was intent on learning such things of the shedim*. It was not often that they were spoken of. This was completely unheard of. He sat listening intently and nodding.

"They begged him not to torture them before the time. He sent them into a herd of swine owned by a wealthy man that had maliciously abused me for years. In my mind it was an act of justice. He released me from the abyssal darkness in which I had been imprisoned my whole life."

"He explained to me about the love and compassion of His Father, Adonai, the God of Abraham, Isaac, and Jacob."

Joseph gulped loudly and shook his head in disbelief. This was a side of his God he had never known. He was in awe of the goodness being related to him.

"He will be crucified as the perfect sacrifice for all humanity. Then as Jonah was in the belly of the fish for 3 days he also will be in the belly of the earth before he is resurrected. This is the news that he told me to tell you."

Joseph sat eyes closed contemplatively for a few minutes then suddenly erupted into extreme loud worship. Theodore was unable to understand his words and assumed it was the language of his people. He watched intently as the old man stood and danced arms raised in worship. This continued for a long while and Theodore joined in the Greek language, until they blended their worship in outrageous laughter.

The Demoniac

Joseph taught Theodore the basics of all he had learned from Torah. In the wee hours of the morning when the moon lit the sky, his servants brought food and wine. It was the finest he had ever tasted.

Every word was absorbed as a delicious morsel bringing strength and health to a weak and feeble soul. He wished Gaios were there to learn from this great man. He told the story from the beginning when God spoke the universe into existence then all life except for humans whom He took the time to form with His own hands creating them in His image. How He breathed life into Adam and Eve and joined them in the garden for daily walks. He told of the evil snake and the trick he played on mankind. He told of the stories of King David and the prophets' words regarding the messiah. He repeated some of the Psalms of David and the Proverbs of the wise King Solomon.

After talking all night, they were both exhausted and Joseph insisted that they sleep there in the tent. Once they woke for the day, Joseph lavished his new friend with the finest foods and wine. He treated his servants with grace and kindness of which Theodore had not previously been exposed. He remained there for three days and nights both learning from one another.

The Demoniac

As he prepared to continue his mission journey, Joseph gave him a donkey loaded with food, wine, and water along with a blanket, and a new set of clothes and sandals. He had not expected anything and was again overcome with gratitude.

The Demoniac

Epilogue

Joseph returned to Capernaum and found his friend Jairus was blessed by Jesus of Nazareth as well. Word was spreading like wildfire across all of Israel and Judah about the man some insisted was the Messiah come to earth in flesh and blood while others whispered about the deception overtaking the weak-minded. Joseph continued doing business in both Capernaum and in Gerasa, growing more prosperous in both body and soul.

While in Capernaum, word reached him that Jesus of Nazareth had been sentenced to death by Roman crucifixion, he left for Jerusalem in order to be a witness on his behalf. Alas, he was too late, and this Messiah was put to death. He had purchased a tomb for his family and was now determined that Jesus was to have it.

Going before Pilate he asked for the body to be given to him prior to sunset which would still be time to give his body dignity and not break the law for High Holy days.

Pilate agreed and word was sent to the Roman soldiers to release the body to Joseph of Arimathea who comforted those at the foot of the cross with the knowledge of a suitable grave.

...The tomb was used for only three days and nights.

Epilogue 2

Theodore made peace with Aspasia, Desma, and Aphrodesia, telling each of them about Jesus. Aphrodesia left the temple and became a devout follower of The Rabbi of Love. He married Aria after spending a full year in search of his childhood sweetheart. She had stayed on the Island of Cyprus.

Once released from the temple of Aphrodite she lived in a small home as a servant to a wealthy woman named Zeta, who gave generously to the ministry of a compassionate prophet named Jesus of Nazareth. Following their wedding they traveled the Decapolis testifying to the greatness of Adonai, the God of the Jews. When Jesus returned to the Decapolis following his resurrection, Aria became intensely dedicated to bringing the good news to everyone along with her husband. The two were not able to have children.

In the years to come Theodore was joined by a zealot named Paul in spreading the Good news of the Way. They saw the harvest of souls daily.

The Demoniac

The Demoniac

Definitions

Peplos: a body-length garment, long tubular cloth with the top edge folded down about halfway, so that what was the top of the tube was at the ankle.

Hetaera; (hetaerae; hetaeros [male] plural); a type of prostitute who served as an artist, entertainer and talker aside from providing sexual services. They were highly educated and allowed in the symposium.

Chiton: a long woolen tunic.

Gymnasium: a place for training by males for physical and mental education.

Bar Mitzva: a religious initiation ceremony of a Jewish boy who has reached the age of 13 and is regarded as ready to observe religious precepts and eligible to take part in public worship.

Iatrine: a midwife

Epiblema: A piece of cloth worn over the peplos or chiton, comparative to a shawl.

Eromenos: An adolescent boy who is the passive partner in a homosexual relationship.

The Demoniac

Erastes: The older, active partner in a homosexual relationship.

Kedeshah: A sacred prostitute who often played an important part in official temple worship. They could be either male or female.

Shedim: Hebrew word for demons or spirits.

Eema: mother

Meaning of Names:

Kataramenos: cursed

Desma: binding oath

Plouton: Wealth; An alternate name for the god of the underworld.

Petros: stone or rock

Aspasia: welcome, invite

Zena: belonging to Zeus

Ponos: Greek god of hard labor

Aria: song or melody; in Hebrew it means lioness

The Demoniac

Cassius: empty or hollow

Theodore: blessing of God

Gaios: to rejoice

The Demoniac

www.ingramcontent.com/pod-product-compliance
Lightning Source LLC
Chambersburg PA
CBHW030251270626
47156CB00021B/1543